DOOMED

To from
_11/26/13_
from Nancy
_NB_

NANCY BEAUDET

iUniverse LLC
Bloomington

DOOMED

This is a work of fiction. All of the characters, names, incidents, organizations, and dialogue in this novel are either the products of the author's imagination or are used fictitiously.

iUniverse books may be ordered through booksellers or by contacting:

iUniverse LLC
1663 Liberty Drive
Bloomington, IN 47403
www.iuniverse.com
1-800-Authors (1-800-288-4677)

ISBN: 978-1-4917-0741-8 (sc)
ISBN: 978-1-4917-0743-2 (hc)
ISBN: 978-1-4917-0742-5 (e)

Library of Congress Control Number: 2013917341

Printed in the United States of America.

iUniverse rev. date: 10/09/2013

For my mom—

I love you.

Thank you for being my best friend.

The course of true love never did run smooth.
—William Shakespeare

Chapter 1

I fought my whole life to keep from becoming one of *those* girls. The kind of girls I always hated vehemently, whether they truly ever deserved it or not.

The kind of girls who tortured me relentlessly in high school and for all the years that led up to it.

The kind of girls to whom having a boyfriend means the world—and not having one means the end of it.

I mean, it's not like I didn't want a boyfriend; a part of me always did, I guess.

Out of curiosity if nothing else.

I had wished for and wondered what kissing would be like, just like every other thirteen-year-old girl. Never, though, not for even a fraction of a second during all those years of imagining and all those years that followed, did I ever come close to imagining what it would *really* be like. How it would feel to fall in love and wade my way through the inevitable pain that comes with such a thing.

The pain of love …

The pain of loss …

Suffering both simultaneously.

A pain so vast and futile it's like a bullet that goes straight through the heart, making the air around me suddenly too difficult to breathe.

The pain of needing someone much more desperately than I had ever given myself permission to.

A pain dulled just as quickly as it appeared, smothered like a flame by a soft kiss to the cheek. Strong arms forever wrapped around me, keeping me warm and safe.

I wish that someone had warned me; I wish that he had just left me alone.

I wish that we had met sooner, and I wish that we had never met at all.

Life doesn't work that way, though.

We don't get everything we ask for. Sometimes we get more.

I was doomed the day I met him ...

Whether I ever realized it or not, for better or for worse, no matter what, trapped in a love story that I couldn't get out of, that I didn't *want* out of, no matter what.

All I can do now is hit rewind and play that fateful day over and over in my head. Torturing myself indefinitely with the reminder of his kind and easy smile, the way his hands fit perfectly around my waist, the day not so long ago, the way he made me feel small and beautiful when he said:

"God, I love you."

I turned around, startled.

My face reddened as the clerk tried to stifle a giggle, feigning a cough as she handed me the bag with my books in it.

"You tripped," he explained.

As if "God, I love you" were the most obvious response there was, his face turning a shade of crimson as he laughed.

"It was cute," he added.

I looked at my shoes, damp from the mud outside. I hated when he did that.

I hated how easily he made my heart thrum and my palms sweat. Once again, I didn't know how or if to respond.

"Thanks?" I mumbled awkwardly, still avoiding his gaze as I moved past him and toward the exit. He lingered close behind, like always. His fingers almost constantly were intertwined with mine—warm, safe, and comforting.

Since there was quite a bit of snow on the ground, we had to walk carefully, Warren's grip tightening here and there, steadying me when I could not steady myself.

He let go only once, when my phone started vibrating violently, followed by the muffled sounds of Taylor Swift belting out her latest hit.

The cliché lyrics "Baby, can't you see/ you belong with me?" filled the silence that lingered between us as my face reddened and Warren laughed.

"Hello?" I very nearly yelled, my voice breathless from the frantic search to the bottom of my purse.

"Emerson? Is that you?"

It was my mom, of course. She sounded just as breathless and confused as I did, if not more so.

"Yeah, of course it's me."

I glanced at Warren, knowing how idiotic I sounded but thankful that he was no longer standing close enough to hear her response.

"Where are you?" she demanded. Her voice was still soft and mother-like, although laced with parental suspicions.

"Are you with Warren? You guys aren't going back to his house, are you?"

I very nearly died, seriously. Right there.

My entire frame swayed back and forth, and I bit my lip and resisted the urge to say, "Yeah, so what if we are?"

Instead, I continued to distance myself from Warren in a handful of steps. I ducked behind my hair and mumbled a quick and almost undecipherable, "Yeah, I think so, why?"

His age.

I knew the thoughts that had entered my mother's head long before she did, as always. Even her breathing gave her away.

Taking a deep breath of my own, I reacted the same way I had been for months now as the words I knew were coming flowed easily from her mouth. Just like I knew they would.

"Honey, wouldn't you just rather come home?" She insisted, without actually insisting that I do so. "I mean, there isn't really even anything for you guys to do at his house, is there?"

I waited, our conversation very nearly dying on that last sentence alone.

What did she want me to say? *Yes, actually, there is. I want more than anything to go back to his house so we can cuddle and kiss on his couch, just as we always do.*

The mere thought of his lips on mine sent a shiver straight down my spine, only ending when it reached my toes.

Should I tell her that being anywhere near him is like an instant high that I just can't get enough of?

I sighed, knowing that I could never tell her any of that. Well, at least not yet anyway, not that it mattered. I found as I glanced over my shoulder at Warren once again that it mattered even less.

"I have to go, okay, Mom?" I sighed, the words coming out half-strangled. "I'll call you later."

I didn't wait for a response, slamming my thumb down on the end-call button as I turned around.

Warren's arms widened as I made my way back toward him through the snow and slush, an irresistible smile playing on the corner of his lips.

"She hates me, doesn't she?" he asked, his face light but his voice serious, tinged with worry and guilt.

I shook my head, my stomach twisting with nerves as the bus pulled up in front of us.

We stepped aside as a few elderly ladies stepped past us and into the snowbank, walkers slow against the slush.

I was unable to stop myself from glancing down at my shoes once more as Warren took my hand and pulled me up the steps behind him.

I kept my head down as he found a seat near the back and pulled me down into a barrage of hugs and kisses. One hand rubbed my arm as the other alternated between stroking my face and playing with my hair.

I blushed, leaning in to him as every cell in my body hoped and prayed that this would never end as every ounce of intuition in my bones fought to tell me otherwise.

Since neither of us were what anyone would dare to call licensed, we were forced to rely on public transportation to get us from point A to point B, which usually meant the distance between Warren's place and mine.

I didn't mind.

Resting my head on the crook of his shoulder, I watched dreamily as the world passed by. Feeling utterly peaceful and safe, I counted stop signs as I listened to Warren's heartbeat.

I wished I could snuggle my way even closer against his chest, though I knew that no matter how close I got, it would never be close enough.

I glanced down at my phone as it vibrated once more, illuminating the inside of my purse in an eerie cobalt glow. Thankfully, I had had enough common sense to turn the ringer off after the last debacle.

It was Alyssa, of course.

Her messages were just as undecipherable as they always were, asking what I was up to and where I was.

It was a true tribute to our friendship that I was able to understand exactly what it was that she wanted, considering that what I read and what I knew she meant seemed to be two completely different things.

Merp u get duin

I laughed, unable to stop myself.

Warren's body shifted at the change in silence as his nose nudged by my ear, his dark eyes finding mine with ease.

I gulped, ducking my head behind my hair, creating a thin shield of blonde between us.

I didn't even have to look up to know what he wanted; his thoughts often displayed openly across his face. He was more often than not—for me at least—very easy to read.

"It's Alyssa," I mumbled, tilting my phone in his direction so that he could see. "Her phone got run over by a truck or something a few weeks ago," I noted, explaining the spelling mistakes.

Still avoiding his eyes but shifting in my seat so that one of my knees now touched his, I sighed. I wanted more than anything to shift so that my legs overlapped his completely.

He snorted, his chest shaking as he let out a quiet laugh. Even though I wasn't sure if he was referring to Alyssa or my not so subtle change in posture, it didn't matter. I loved the sound regardless.

My heart thrummed once more as his fingers traced circles on my palm. His hands massaged my thumb to my middle finger and readjusted my hand until I was flipping him off and holding it there, just as he had done a million and one times before. It still made me laugh.

It was not until he dislodged himself from my grasp and began pulling away that I realized it was almost time for us to get off. I had been so wrapped up in his presence that I had failed to notice as he reached back to pull the bell.

I stood with caution, holding my bag against my shoulder as his hand once again found mine.

The bus threw us forward as it came to an abrupt stop against the curb, causing me to stumble awkwardly into Warren's back, my hands reaching out for anything that I could grasp, unable to stop myself as I fell forward.

I was unable to be graceful even when I wanted to most. I blushed as an older woman eyed me nervously; I felt my face flush bright red.

Warren just laughed, his face lighting up as he gripped me tighter, pulling me to him and securing me against his side.

Once again he steadied me when I was unable to steady myself.

The walk to Warren's apartment, a large white building decorated with dozens of windows on either side, didn't take very long.

I felt a rush of unease as I followed him up the concrete steps that led to the front door. I was still somewhat uncomfortable with the fact that I was going into a boy's home.

Alone.

A boy who was not even really a boy at all, what with the five-year head start he had on me, not to mention the beard and silky black ponytail that ended in ringlet curls halfway down his back.

Warren definitely was not what anyone could consider a *boy*. In reality, he was a *man*.

His looks were only one of the many reasons our sudden friendship had not come with the greatest of responses.

I was the good girl. The girl who had never been kissed.

He was my opposite.

We weren't supposed to fit.

"What?" Warren asked, unlocking the door to apartment 107 and noticing my discomfort, like he always did.

"Nothing." I lied.

I smiled in an effort to appear smooth, natural. As if I were used to this kind of thing, as if even before him I had done this kind of thing countless times before. I knew deep down that much to my dismay, he already knew me far too well to ever believe any of that.

Maybe that was a good thing.

Chapter 2

Warren's apartment was small, but always much cleaner than I expected it to be.

Despite the ever-growing stack of video games that usually covered the living room table from end to end. Despite the floor littered with dust-covered systems, cords, and plugs, like a map indented into the carpet.

The walls were adorned with little more than a small plaque that his mother had undoubtedly placed above the kitchen sink. The words *No place like home* stared back at me in all of their pink cliché glory.

As I looked around, I could not help but notice that nothing had changed much in the week since I had been over last.

An array of water bottles and energy drinks still littered the kitchen counter.

Warmth streamed in openly through the large balcony doors, pushed open just enough for us to hear the torrid details of his neighbor's affair with the woman hired to keep the garden in fresh and working order.

My eyes darted from the counter to Warren's back as I laughed.

I slipped off my shoes and kicked them toward the old black mat that lingered between the carpet and the linoleum. The toes of my boots were soaked right through, drenching my socks.

The bit of unease grew as I reached back to close the door behind me.

His broad shoulders were a stark contrast against my more feminine frame. Not that my frame was really all that feminine to begin with, what with me not really being the kind of girl anyone would describe as *petite*.

Still, my shoulders barely made up half the width of Warren's. His large hands were more than able to fully envelop mine the way they would a small child's.

I felt my cheeks redden as I was reminded of another one of the many reasons I fell for him in the first place.

He always made me feel small, and as a girl who had spent most if not all of her life being called every variation of the word *fat,* well, let's just say making me feel small and not like the overweight outcast I always seemed to be wasn't something that could be accomplished easily.

I watched as he ducked through the entryway that led to the kitchen, pulling off his winter jacket and dropping it onto the same kitchen chair that he always did.

The sound shook me from my reverie as he turned to smile at me, making me laugh as always with just a single look.

Was it possible for someone so robust to be so smooth and graceful?

He closed the distance between us in only a handful of steps, dark eyes easy on mine. Then he took me into his arms with ease, his fingers clasping together against my lower back.

The dark strands of his hair spilled over his shoulder, like silk when it brushed up against my skin,

A smile played at the corner of his lips as he pushed my *own* hair back behind my ears, eyes bright, excited.

"You're all red," he whispered, leaning down so that we were nose to nose, chin to chin.

His gaze was so intense that I felt the need to back up a little, if only to look away and find my breath once again, my thoughts as incoherent as they had ever been.

"It's cute," Warren said again and laughed quietly.

His lips were cold against my nose, and his eyes bore into mine, searching their depths as his lips loomed in heavily against mine, making sure that this was okay.

I nodded breathlessly, my hands clasped against the back of his neck.

Every bit of unease was forgotten the second his lips pressed slowly against mine, parting slightly.

I loved him.

That was the only thing that I could think of, that I loved this. Even if I didn't truly know it yet, I think that he did.

My hands tangled in his hair as legs fought against gravity, eager to wrap themselves around his waist and hold him to me.

Warren's hands, soft and strong, began to roam freely from my head and down to my toes, knowing my limits and never forcing his way past them. Not even for a second.

"You okay?" he asked, lips against my jaw, my neck, my nose, and any part of skin that he could see and reach.

I nodded, pulling him forward so that every inch of my body pressed tightly against his.

His grip became tighter against my legs as he lifted me up against the sink, every inch of my body even with his, his lips never leaving mine.

I suddenly could not remember a time when I did not need *this*. Need *him*. The thought alone scared me more than anything else.

"What?" Warren asked, his breath warm against my cheek as I felt myself begin to pull away. I shrugged, looking down as I played a loose string from the shoulder of his T-shirt.

"Nothing." I tried to laugh and smile, but the sound was incomplete.

Even so, Warren didn't seem to notice—or if he did, he didn't mention it.

His returning smile was just as warm as it ever was as his forehead touched mine.

I sighed as he helped me down.

He held my hand tight in his as we made our way to the darkened living room. The drapes were drawn the way they always were, barely allowing even the smallest sliver of natural light into the room.

"God you're like a vampire," I teased, making my way past the suede couch and two leather chairs that had been placed on either side of the living room table.

Pulling the blinds back, I gazed outside. There wasn't much to see. A balcony full of leaves and a few stray joggers chasing down their runaway toddlers in the park across the street—the usual Riverside attractions. Nothing more; nothing less.

"Come on," Warren said.

I felt his warmth against my back, his lips at my neck, my ear, my jaw, my cheek.

"Come cuddle with me," he said.

It was impossible to say no; even if I had wanted to, I could not even remember the word or the meaning that lay behind it.

The words *come cuddle with me* were impossible to resist.

I was terrified.

Laughter shook his chest as his warm arms wrapped firmly and protectively around my waist, holding me against his heart and keeping me there.

Unable to think, unable to breathe, I had no idea what to do next, no idea how to react.

My mind was unable to retrace the steps between my lips and his. It clouded with a lust-induced coma as his fingers traced circles against my skin.

"What?" he asked without really needing to do so.

"Nothing." I lied.

I forced myself to turn so that I was almost facing him. We were on the couch then, even though I had been no help whatsoever in us getting there.

His head hit the pillow with a soft thud as he pulled me forward, straddling him, our feet now tangled, his warm hands on my back.

"You're hurt," Warren suddenly said.

His voice startled me, sounding *sad* of all things.

"You have a line of hurt on your head," he explained as I shifted so that I was able to fully look him in the eye.

All the while letting Warren's hand guide mine through my hair, I felt around for any sort of injury. His hands taking there sweet time along my skull, the feeling of his skin against mine vibrating my insides.

When I finally found a small cut, I had no explanation for how it had gotten there.

That wasn't a surprise. *I'm good at getting hurt.*

Any day when I did not come home with a bruise or a scrape, without having dropped or broken anything, was a good day for me. This unfortunately didn't happen very often.

"That's nothing." I shrugged, laughing as if he should know this by now, should know me by now.

Warren didn't laugh, though. The feel of his lips in my hair made me blush.

"I don't like it," Warren explained, without needing to; it was evident in his voice, his touch. He didn't like it when I got hurt. He never had.

He wouldn't even let me use scissors or a knife whenever he was around to stop me.

I wished for his sake that was the only danger we had to worry about, the only kind of pain, the silly meaningless kind.

I would have taken a thousand punches and kicks if it would have meant protecting him and what we had. That kind of hurt heals slowly and with time. Heartbreak, though, that kind of pain never goes away.

Chapter 3

It was dark outside by the time my mother phoned. The sound of my cell phone going off was enough to make both of us jump. The calm serenity of his dark living room had instantly evaporated with the sound.

Warren smiled, holding his new position above me with ease, his arms placed sturdily on either side of my face.

He seemed to be shielding my body with his own. What exactly he was shielding me from, I don't think I will ever know.

All I know is I felt safe there. My socked feet twisted in and around his. My hands soothed their way down from his neck to his chest and all the way back again.

I had never felt so safe in my entire life. Shifting so that my body pressed firmly against his, I lifted myself and surveyed the floor with my one free hand, feeling around for my bag. My phone still buzzed noisily.

It had been like this almost every night for months now. The summer leaves had been replaced quickly with faded grass and ice-coated sidewalks. His fingers were constantly intertwined with mine—warm, safe, and comforting.

Warren and I were always entangled on his couch, and my mom always called at ten o'clock to let me know she had come to fetch me.

I was like a tennis ball waiting anxiously, scanning the grounds for the next available dog, frozen and in limbo.

It's not that my mom didn't like Warren; she did, I'm sure.

I was her baby, though, and having your baby spending every single second with an older boy doing God knows what (which in our reality was really nothing) is probably every mother's worst nightmare.

"I have to go," I said, nearly falling to the floor with my phone now in hand.

Warren grabbed me easily enough. He set me back against the pillows and between his arms.

"Nope," he announced simply, crushing me with all of his weight until I found it hard to breathe.

I wondered briefly if these were the kinds of moves that wrestlers used to win a match; they had the same effect.

I turned my phone to unlock the screen and held it behind his head. The text message *here no rush* glowed back at me.

No rush. It was so tempting to take her seriously, to stay like this for a few more minutes. *Oh, if only she were serious.*

I, however, knew differently.

The ride home would be just as quiet as it always was.

Me, a blushing insane head case that was practically bouncing up and down in the seat next to her.

My mother, my best friend for all intents and purposes, whom I was so used to telling everything to, did not want to know anything about this. At least not the parts that were supposed to lead to something else, something bigger, something I wasn't quite ready to comprehend.

"I have to," I whispered, locking lips with Warren once again, distracting him long enough to free myself enough to sit up properly.

"When you working?" His voice was sad and pleading once again.

It was the same question he always asked when I left, as if he needed to know when he would see me again. Not knowing simply was not acceptable. It was a feeling that I could definitely relate to.

"Ten thirty, I think." I shrugged, trying to force a smile as I fumbled around in the darkness.

I didn't want to think about what the next day would bring. Warren was unequivocally the only thing about work that held any interest for me whatsoever anymore. Everything else, *everyone* else, was just a distraction, a voice or an insult echoing in the background.

To say that people had not taken *kindly* to me and Warren was the understatement of the century, but more so somehow.

It had almost been two years since we'd both started work at Tagman's, the largest (and only) grocery emporium in Riverside.

The two of us had started only three months apart. We walked past each other every day without so much as a hello or glance passing between us.

I had noticed him, of course. The long dark curls of his hair were almost impossible to miss in a crowd of blond buzz cuts and pimply faced sixteen-year-olds. I unfortunately was one of those pimply faced sixteen-year-olds. Warren, though, he was something else.

He was an adult, a man.

He terrified me.

"Hey, Em!" one of his friends had yelled one day, Warren not far behind.

It was impossible not to notice how big they both were.

The one who had spoken had to be at least two heads taller than I was, if not more so. His shoulders were more than twice the size of Warren's and mine combined.

His brown hair jutting out this way and that, he, like the rest of the truck unloaders, often looked like he'd just jumped out of bed.

What is with these guys? I could remember thinking. *They never go anywhere alone!*

I could remember being afraid.

No one ever called my name out that way without something to say behind it.

His smile, sick and twisted, was not reassuring in the least.

"What?" I shot back, not even bothering to be polite about it. I folded my arms across my chest as I waited for whatever insult he was about to dish out. I was used to this.

They stopped a few feet from where I stood, eyes wide and defensive, ready for attack. They were laughing just enough to send shock waves of panic up and down my spine.

"Warren likes you," the boy beside Warren choked out in a fit of hysterical laughter.

I finally remembered his name was Caleb.

If I had not already disliked him, the feeling was now stronger than ever. Now the feeling was closer to hate.

"Go fuck yourself." I spat the words out like venom, which was exactly how they were supposed to come out.

Still, I would have been lying to myself if I said I had not noticed the way Warren's smile suddenly vanished. It was replaced instantly by a look that could only be described as one thing.

Hurt.

Warren touched my hand then, shaking me from my reverie. I realized that I should probably go.

He walked me slowly to the door, where once again his lips met mine, so soft and sweet that it was almost maddening.

I found myself wondering once again, as I often did in his presence, how had I ever lived without this? Without him?

Would I ever be able to again?

It was pathetic really how easily I knew the answer, how loud it echoed inside my head.

No, with a capital N.

Chapter 4

Once outside I found I could finally breathe, could finally think clearly. The icy wind bit at my flushed cheeks as I ran down the slope of his front yard toward the only vehicle parked on the abandoned street.

My mom merely glanced up as I jumped in, smiling slightly as the light that popped on when I opened the door illuminated how tired she was.

My guilt began to radiate—guilt for keeping her out so late, guilt for making her wait. "Sorry," I mumbled pathetically. My face flushed with heat, so at odds with the frosty world outside.

"It's okay." She sighed. She shifted the old blue van into drive, tired eyes focused only on the road ahead.

I sat there a fidgety, nervous, overheated mess. I longed to tell her everything but was at a complete loss as to how. I knew that there was no way for her to understand something that I didn't even understand myself.

We drove the rest of the way home in silence, with little aside from the radio to fill the air that hung heavily between us.

The desperate cries of one desperate pop star did little to overshadow the misery of his duet partner. Her voice came out half-strangled as she did her best to radiate as much passion as he radiated a sad lack of self-confidence.

My mind and pulse raced like a complete head case.

My phone buzzed against my hands before we were even around the corner and continued to do so once we were long past it.

The words *come back now* were enough to make every bone in my body ache. Oh, how I wanted to.

Instead, I tucked my phone facedown in my pocket. Out of sight, out of mind.

Ha! As if.

My dad was asleep by the time we got home, the house quiet and dark.

My mom's keys dropping heavily onto the wooden table was the only sound for miles.

"Good night," she called as I bounded my way down the old wooden stairs that connected my cave with the rest of the house.

I dropped my purse onto the floor as I searched for my pajamas. My alarm clock was now showing almost 10:30.

My head filled with one thought and one thought only: *I do not want to work tomorrow.*

I did not want to face what I knew I would face the second the bus pulled up alongside the old worn-out curb that led to the Tagman's grocery emporium, otherwise known as minimum-wage, blue-vested hell.

It was almost enough to make me nostalgic for the smell of chalkboards and prepubescent hormones that lingered along the halls of Riverside High School.

No one there seemed to care about Warren and me and whatever it was that we meant to each other.

The older boy so seemingly taken with a girl so opposite of what he appeared to be, what people desperately wanted him to be, people who did not want *him* to be with *me*.

The girl so much the opposite of what they *expected* me to be.

Pushing back the blankets, I forced myself to breathe, repeating the lyrics "Better stand tall when they're calling you out; don't bend, don't break, baby, don't back down" in my head.

I glanced down at my tattoo as I tucked myself in; it was a cross holding a rose.

The words *It's my life* were forever etched into my skin, my own personal reminder that, *yes, I* can *do this.*

I could only hope as I glanced at my phone one last time, Warren's words glowing against the darkness, that I truly believed it.

Chapter 5

I couldn't remember the first time that her words had struck a chord.

The girl whose fullest and cruelest intent settled on my love life, dead set and aimed. The sound of a phone ringing loudly against hollow walls was so normal that it faded easily into the background.

"Emerson, it's for you," someone called, although I never really noticed who; the soft voice failed to stand out, seemingly kind words echoing against the walls.

The break room was just as loud as ever; voices that should have pounded against my skull seemed to do little but echo in the background.

The words *something about your boyfriend* were all I heard, standing out in an array of voices. All were ready and eager for the same thing: *escape.* I think it was a Monday, the clock showing almost eight. The last few hours of a night shift left to linger desperately.

I got up without a second thought and dropped my vest onto one of the cleaner tables that filled an otherwise disastrous break room— tables and chairs coated in long-forgotten jackets and clothes.

I can remember laughing at something Trevor said as he stumbled somewhat drunkenly toward the time clock. I'm almost completely sure that he was (and usually is) completely sober, almost.

His words, "See you later, fancy pants," echoed down the hallway as he yelled, the sound of his feet shuffling against concrete lasting long after he was gone.

I was laughing as I picked up the phone, distracted and unthinking. I was sure that it was just Tommy, my "supervisor" for all intents and purposes, phoning to let me know that I was late—again—and using Warren as an excuse to get me to answer. Instead, I felt the floor give way completely, the walls collapsing around me, leaving me alone and paralyzed, unable to think or breathe.

"You know that Warren would sleep with anything, right?"

I froze, unable to think or move, my lips forming words that made no sense in my head, my heart pounding furiously against my chest.

"Who the hell is this?" I demanded, my words sounding choked and weak, even to me. Tears threatened to overwhelm me completely as wetness soaked my eyelashes and burned against my cheeks.

"It's Rebecca." She laughed—seriously laughed, *as if any of this was funny, as if any of it made sense.*

Anger flared dangerously in my veins. My skin was suddenly hot with a fury unlike any I had felt before.

It was fury with Warren. His dark eyes burning bright in the back of my mind, a smile kinder than I had ever known, suddenly seemed sinister, twisted easily by the words of a single girl, a girl I barely even knew.

My fists clenched at the sound of her voice.

"Yeah," she continued, her voice taking on a tone filled with glee and laughter, holding my bruised and bleeding heart out in the open for the entire world to see.

"He was just out in the garden center with me and Janelle, and he said that you're nothing special and that he would sleep with anything—he was just desperate."

Just desperate.

Her words echoed in my head, vibrating painfully against my skull.

He was *just desperate.*

"Just desperate enough to want to sleep with me?" I wanted to scream.

Instead, I slammed the phone against the wall with all the restraint that I could manage, which considering everything, wasn't much.

My mind refused to think clearly as I made my way clumsily from the break room and down the hall.

I grasped at the walls as my feet seemed to go numb beneath me. I still couldn't breathe. Tears now flowed freely down my cheeks.

Warm hands on my skin pulled me backward and into someone's arms.

His arms.

His voice was laced with worry as he tried desperately to hold me against his chest.

Every bone in my body fought to get away. "Let me go," I cried, pushing against Warren with all the strength that I could muster.

Every touch was like the prick of a needle, every kiss a kick straight to the chest. Never in my life had I felt pain like this.

"I *know* what you said, okay?" I found myself suddenly screaming. "Rebecca told me you said you would sleep with anything and that I was nothing special."

The words burned at my insides, leaving my vocal chords singed and scarred. "You were just desperate enough to *want* to sleep with me."

I spat the words out like venom. Every memory was now tainted and stained.

The boy who only moments earlier had been the *one* person I trusted most in the world, the *one* person who I thought would always love me no matter what, stared painfully back at me.

"You know me," was all he said. "You know me."

He was right, of course.

I *did* know him, the real him. I just had no idea how well yet.

His temper flared dangerously as he walked away from me, his hands clenched into fists.

My thoughts never strayed toward Rebecca, knowing that he would never hurt her, that he would never hurt a woman, no matter what, despite how much she might have deserved it.

I never thought, not even for a fraction of a second, that the boy who was much too shy to talk to even the pizza guy could be seen as not only scary but as truly terrifying.

My eyes had long since run dry after spending God knows how long alone and broken on the cold bathroom floor.

My phone, easily forgotten, vibrated loudly against the linoleum, glowing with messages that I did not care to read.

Finally I forced myself to stand, waiting until whatever customers had wandered in to do their business had hacked, coughed, grunted, and washed their hands.

I made my way slowly back toward the scene of the crime, my hair forming a blonde shield around my tearstained cheeks.

It was only then that I heard him. I heard Warren.

His voice was raised in an anger that bounced easily off the poorly painted walls that surrounded him.

"What is wrong with you?" he screamed, his fury so strong that it was almost tangible. "You're nothing! Do you hear me? Nothing!"

I froze.

"You stay away from Emerson, do you understand me? You ever go anywhere near her again, you ever talk to her again, I will rip your fucking throat out."

Other voices began to interject themselves.

Strong arms were holding him back as I crossed the distance that lingered between us.

"Come on, Warren, that's enough, okay? That's enough," Joel grumbled.

His gray face laced with stress, Warren didn't seem to hear him. His eyes were nearly bloodred.

"Stay away from her."

The words bounded around the room. They echoed back at me, piercing my skin.

Rebecca's eyes met mine for the slightest of seconds before she made her way slowly past me, a monster turned to stone.

She was gone before I could react.

My hands reached for Warren's. His skin was red and hot beneath my fingertips as he pulled angrily away from me.

"I'm sorry" was all I could say, my words limp and useless. I knew all the while that believing her words was something I would never be able to take back.

The memory was like a nightmare, lingering in the back of my mind as my eyes opened to another day, gray and tainted.

My alarm buzzed noisily as my body refused to move, my legs numb beneath my sheets.

Beep beep beep.

The blankets were a warm comfort in contrast with what I knew today would surely bring. My mind was filled with one thought only: *I do not want to work today.*

It was still snowing outside by the time I finally got upstairs. My hair was damp from the shower. The sound of NASCAR welcomed me from the living room as my dad sat happily in the green chair that he had long since claimed as *his.*

"Hey, brat-face," he called, his use of my favorite nickname confirming his good mood.

My mom's tired eyes met mine over a plate filled with eggs and sausage. It was my dad's favorite breakfast, ready and waiting to be served.

"Hey, honey." She smiled, tank top haphazardly tucked into a pair of pale green pajama pants.

"How's Bigfoot?" my dad called. He had to yell to be heard over the sound of Jeff Gordon's latest triumph.

"He's good, Dad." I laughed, wondering all the while if he actually knew Warren's name or not.

I knew deep down that the preferred option for *any* father would be to refer to the man whose true intent he was *sure* was violating his youngest daughter, as a mythical creature, a monster lurking in the woods.

I could not help but laugh as I found myself unable to forget the first time that such a creature had come in contact with the person he feared most of all—my father.

At five foot six with a haircut that closely resembled Shrek's and a heart bigger than Donald Trump's ego, my father wasn't exactly someone to strike fear into the hearts of men at first glance.

The cold memory bit at me. Warren's sweaty hands had been so tight on mine as his face twisted with terror. Even so, every time Warren touched me, it set my skin on fire. Even as we sat somewhat alone in the back of my parents' old blue van, the engine revving against the cold.

As my mom made her way toward the house, which sat surrounded on all sides by snow-covered pine trees, our breath mixed in the frosty air that hung heavily between us.

"Relax." I had laughed, unable to hide my amusement.

"Dude!" Warren had more or less squealed as my dad neared the driveway where we sat, concealed by frost-covered windows.

"Dude, he is so going to kill me," Warren pursued.

What Warren had done that deserved a death sentence was truly beyond me.

My laughter only increased as my dad's hands found the door with ease, yanking it toward him and exposing us to the cold.

"Hey, Bigfoot." My dad had smiled, grabbing Warren's clammy hand in his the way a rattlesnake grabs a rabbit.

Warren's entire face flooded with relief as he smiled. Still somewhat anxious, he said, "Hey, how are you?"

They were talking before either my mom or I could keep up.

The latest hockey game provided gossip, which neither of us cared to understand.

Instead, I sat back happily.

Happy that the boy with the ponytail seemed to fit in so well with the man who would have happily pulled out his shotgun if necessary.

"What do you want for breakfast?" my mom asked, unknowingly pulling me back toward her from that cold, frosty day, interrupting my daydreams with a the scent of pancakes and syrup. Her head was already ducked inside the freezer as she searched for my favorite kind of waffles.

As I ate my waffles topped with syrup and peanut butter, warmer memories forced their way through my veins, memories of a man just crazy enough to come up with such a delicious breakfast combination.

Dark eyes were wide as he beamed back at me, this man whom I tried desperately not to think of or about. Every memory was painful of a presence that had long since vanished.

Dark eyes so different from the eyes I stared into now, the tired eyes of his older sister. Her hair frazzled as she moved hurriedly from one burner to the next.

Photographs brimming along the walls surrounded the kitchen counters, photographs of her smiling little brother.

Eyes kind as he had teased me, time and time again, his forehead all wrinkled with laughter and curly black hair.

His every smile full of love and laughter was nothing more than a painful reminder that he was not coming back, not now, not ever.

Chapter 6

It was already a nuthouse by the time I got to work, of course.

Blue carts were scattered across the snow-covered parking lot, the chaos left behind by people eager to start their Christmas shopping, people willing and ready to push anyone and everyone out of their way to do so.

Plugging my headphones into my iPod, I turned the volume up. Loud.

I was eager to drown out the sound of crying infants and parents far too busy texting to do anything about it.

I pushed my way through the throngs of people as I made my way toward the back.

I narrowly avoided being run over by a group of teenagers decked out from head to toe in the latest trend.

Justin Beaver anyone?

No?

Don't blame yah.

"Hey, wait! Em, wait."

I turned unwillingly at the sound of my name. The voice was so at odds with the impatient words that swirled in the air around my head. Alyssa's blonde hair bounced as she ran, cheeks reddened from the cold.

"Hey, girly girl."

I couldn't help but smile as she bounced to a stop in front of me.

I had known Alyssa nearly my whole life.

Blue eyes familiar with glee, she smiled happily back at me, her backpack sagging toward the ground.

"You just starting?" I asked.

"Yeah, ten thirty, you?"

"Same," I sighed, glancing at my phone.

I knew Warren was asleep, but was unable to stop myself from checking anyway.

Every text was a small reassurance I was not alone.

I could get through this.

I *would* get through this.

I had to believe that.

Rebecca's snakelike eyes found me the second Alyssa and I pushed our way toward the lockers through the large blue doors that led to the break room.

The words *Staff Only* screamed back at me in all of their faded red glory.

Every memory of that day's violence was in the back of my mind: Rebecca's eyes on my eyes, her laughter vibrating against my skull, Warren's voice full of a rage that I myself could not comprehend.

Rebecca had barely spoken to me since. The smirk that set easily into her self-tanned skin reminded me that maybe that wasn't such a bad thing after all.

Dropping my purse to the floor, I knelt toward my locker, twisting the numbers this way and that and back again.

Alyssa's voice echoed in the background as Rebecca's eyes silently burned venomous holes in my back.

The latest Tagman's gossip did little to hold my attention as my lock finally clicked into submission. The small blue door banged open with all the subtlety of a hand grenade.

The slightest feeling of relief rushed through me as I realized that my so-called locker mate must be absent today. With a pair of shoes larger than the man's ego himself, he wasn't exactly one to be missed easily. Not that he was all bad.

Not really.

I could have been forced to share lockers with the snake. I could imagine how that dose of venomous revenge would taste.

"Can I have cashier Emerson and cashier Lyssa to the front please? That's cashier Emerson and cashier Lyssa to the front." Tom's voice echoed over the intercom.

Alyssa's glance met mine as she rolled her eyes. A voice far more aggravating than Rebecca's was filling the room, demanding our attention as a head full of dark curls bounced up and down.

Are we having fun yet?

I almost smacked her, seriously.

Evelyn's laughter, loud and obnoxious, echoed against the thin wooden walls, her face creasing as she smiled.

Everything about her set my nervous system on edge; I waited somewhat patiently for her to pounce.

Like moviegoers glued to the edge of their seats, waiting for the villain to strike.

She had a voice not unlike that of the Wicked Witch of the West.

"What time are you *supposed* to start?" she sneered, obviously having heard Tom's not-so-friendly reminder.

She glanced at her watch as her eyes did a total examination of my outfit from my head down to my toes. Black sweatshirt, black T-shirt that clashed against not-so-black sweatpants and dark gray boots.

None of which matched the dress code, of course. My dark blonde hair tied back into a loose ponytail luckily concealed my reddened cheeks in waves.

Her own white collared shirt was neatly pressed and tucked into dark blue polyester pants that stretched to the limit as she bent over time and time again.

"I'm starting *right now,* Evelyn," I shot back, my voice full of annoyance; I didn't care whether she noticed or not.

Alyssa followed closely behind as I made my way toward the time clock. We ignored Evelyn's, "Well, excuse me, then!"

As I swiped my badge, I kept my eyes focused on the doors ahead. I knew that the image of her with her nose in the air as she spoke would only enrage me further.

"Ugh, someone just slap her already, like seriously," Alyssa mumbled, echoing my thoughts completely.

We made it up front just in time for the true madness to begin. Lines twisted in and around clothing racks, and toddlers screamed alongside angry old men and women.

Alyssa's amused eyes met mine as she gripped my hand in hers, holding tightly to a permanent high five.

Both of us heaved heavy sighs as the classic fairy-tale chant burned vividly in the back of my mind: "High-ho, high-ho, off to hell, I go."

Both of us were quickly consumed, separated by space and energy.

I pushed my way through a lineup that had started to resemble a mosh pit, ignoring the elbows that sought to incapacitate me completely.

I was still somewhat unsure of what it was that I was supposed to be doing. Having been a cashier for only a few weeks, I was still unused to the screaming and beeping frenzy.

"Come on now. I got places to be," an angry voice yelled.

My hands fumbled against the keyboard as a line swarmed in front of me, groceries were stacked this way and that, and eggs teetered on the edge of disaster near the magazine rack.

Every fiber of my being was suddenly desperate for the quiet sanctuary of the milk cooler, surrounded by little aside from yellow plastic crates. Oh, why oh why, did I have to go and fall for a truck unloader?

A woman's voice, much kinder than the ones that had surrounded me at the cash register, echoed painfully against my brain, pulling me backward and shoving the reasoning for where I was now right smack-dab in my face. Pale green eyes bore deeply into mine.

As I sat terrified and uncomfortable in the manager's office, my mind replayed everything and anything I could have done in the past twenty-four hours that warranted a firing.

My thoughts settled on one thing and one thing only, the one thing more than capable of turning my entire world completely upside down, more than anything else: Warren.

"We're going to have to move you to the front end." Lorena shrugged, coughing slightly against the silence that followed, her bright yellow *assistant manager* badge glowing green in the fluorescent lighting.

All the benefits of climbing the Tagman's ladder were displayed depressingly in front of me, from the pale green-and-yellow walls to the old office chair that squealed as she readjusted herself every now and again.

Her freshly pressed dress pants were so at odds with my dust-stained sweatpants.

Her heels tapped gently against the old wooden desk, which held little more than a secondhand computer and a few pens.

"Unfortunately we just don't have the full-time hours right now to give to full-time associates like yourself."

Not enough hours? Ha!

What was this?

It had to be some kind of code for "there just isn't enough time in an eight-hour shift for you to gawk at your boyfriend while he pulls skid after skid after skid of dry old Tagman's crap, hair and sweat-covered muscles rippling through his black collared shirt."

Oh, boy!

I forced myself to snap out of it.

I had to concentrate, her words having had little if any impact on my distracted brain cells.

Her eyes were heavy with mascara, and she left words unsaid, knowing all the while that she was right. There would never be enough time in the world for Warren's dark eyes to find mine as he watched me protectively from receiving, ready to run at a moment's notice. Sure, it was only a matter of time before I wiped out and took down a stack of frozen pizzas.

All the while, I knew that she was right: there would never be enough hours in the day, in the week even!

Not enough hours for the sound of his laughter to fill the room, for Warren's six-foot frame stretched to its limits as he reached easily past me, strong arms forming a solid cage of protection around my head as he lifted bottles of broken glass carefully down and set them as far away from me as he could get.

I stared back at Lorena with all the fury that I could manage, my anger thawed somewhat by building anxiety.

Fear of people, fear of change, fear of confrontation—all those fears burned wildly inside of me, for there was nothing I feared more at the time than the so-called front end, the doors of hell.

Managers were paged this way and that for immediate customer assistance.

Furious shoppers ranted and raved angrily about this and that, faces turning tomato-red as they explained repeatedly that they just did not understand *why they couldn't just take their cart of groceries home and pay for it later!*

I knew right then that I was doomed—in more ways than one.

Lorena's words seared themselves against my memory as I grabbed toys and soup cans this way and that, quickly losing track of time.

My phone interrupted my thoughts as it vibrated against my pocket, glowing blue against my vest.

The words *I'm awake where are you?* sent shivers up and down my spine; every fiber of my being longed to be exactly where he was right now, hair flat from sleep, dark eyes scanning the darkness.

I was sure that he was absolutely blind without his glasses.

Strong arms would show through his gray tank top; blue pajama pants would be pulled nearly all the way to his chin. He looked like a sexy old man aging far too fast, despite the fact that he had just only turned twenty-one.

His birthday had passed by in a blur, celebrated long before we had ever really gotten the chance to know each other, before his home had started to feel like my own.

I was unable to stop myself from smiling like an idiot as I maneuvered my pocket until my vest was nearly pulled sideways.

I did my best to text with one hand, ignoring the disapproving grunts of the old woman standing idly next to the debit machine, her hemorrhoid cream still sitting gently on the scanner.

At wordsk.

After three times of hitting the backspace, I gave up, smiling ruefully at my lineup. But I was unable to stop myself from checking every three seconds to see if he had replied yet.

The woman's grumbling lasted until long after she was gone, walker squeaking against the linoleum.

I barely noticed.

My mind was distracted once again.

I was completely consumed by Warren's presence even though he was well out of arm's reach; my phone glowing blue against the inside pocket of my polyester vest kept me constantly aware of him.

I be there soon, goona shower now.

He messaged.

Love n stuff

If my entire sense of concentration wasn't completely screwed beforehand, it sure was now.

His words were nearly enough to send me over the edge completely as I found myself wondering once again how I was ever going to live without this. *Without him.*

The thought alone scared me more than anything else, the answer once again vibrating painfully against my brain. The word echoing against my skull was *No*, with a capital N.

The rest of the day passed easily in a blur of large blue shopping carts and haphazardly packed shopping bags, and crying infants and parents demanding this and that.

My feet were heavy against the tile as I made my way through the crowds and toward the back, sure that at least four days had passed since I reported to work this morning.

Desperate for a break from the frantic space and energy, my eyes met Alyssa's for the briefest of instants—just long enough for her to roll her eyes at the growing line of complainers that had formed directly in front of her.

I couldn't help but smile.

My thoughts once again turned toward my phone. I no longer even bothered to hide it as I checked desperately for the slightest of signs of even one message.

Just one.

That was all I needed to keep going, to keep sane.

Just one reminder that I wasn't alone, that no one had gotten to him yet.

That no one had gotten to me yet.

The witch hunt formed against us was constantly gaining speed as they gathered their gavels and sharpened their switchblades. Their daggers were aimed and ready.

My heart plummeted into my stomach as my search for hope and reassurance came up empty. I knew how ridiculous I was being, but I was unable to find a way around it.

The snakelike eyes of a tormenter that otherwise rarely stood out among the rest followed me as I sighed heavily to myself, clutching my phone tight against my chest.

Her anger with me was far greater than even I could understand.

The hours ticked painfully by as I waited.

Warren's shift did not start for at least another hour or so, and it would not end until long after I was asleep. My desperate need to see him was already much more pathetic than I would ever be ready to admit.

Chapter 7

I found my way to the back in a daze, settling into one of the far corners.

Head down, hair shielding my face, I ignored the glances that seemed to be directed my way, smirks set deep into the skin of those unable or simply unwilling to look away.

Exhaustion threatened to overtake me completely as the frantic energy began to fade away, wearing at my eyelids.

I barely noticed Joel until he was standing right in front of me. His gray beard was lined with grease and sweat, his blue eyes overly kind as he stood obliviously in front of me, smiling like an idiot.

Every fiber of my being was suddenly overtaken by the sudden urge to reach out and slap him, just a little. Just once.

My eyes drifted toward possible weapons and settled on a pair of tweezers, sure to have been left out by one of the night-crew staffers unaware of the fact that self-grooming should only be done where one's self resides, as opposed to where the rest of us are supposed to eat.

I mumbled a quick hello as I picked up my phone and began scrolling mindlessly through day-old Facebook updates.

"So, you and Warren, huh?" he started, plaid shirt pressed and tucked perfectly. He ignored my nonresponse and continued, "Yeah, I told him, you know you got to be careful. You can't be chasing after all these girls anymore if you got one. I'm sure he wouldn't want you to find out about all that, would he? Can't imagine that would go over well."

It was amazing how helpful he could come across while basically saying every rude thing he could think of in just a few sly sentences. It took everything I had in me not to lunge. Seriously, I was tired of this game before it even began.

Joel's knowledge of Warren's and my relationship was about as limited as his knowledge of an actual relationship with any woman able to walk without the assistance of a walker, also known as his mother.

"Thanks, Joel, but I got it, and we're good. Thanks," I sneered as sarcastically as possible without actually being sarcastic.

I glanced at my phone as the seconds of my fifteen-minute break began to tick more and more painfully by. I kept waiting for Joel to get the hint and to get up and out of my face already.

Although his shift didn't start until well after Warren's, he was already here, already dressed proudly in his perfectly pressed blue polyester vest. He smiled at me as he unpacked his backpack, oblivious to my growing resentment.

It was a true tribute to self-control that none of the truck unloaders had strangled him yet, what with his mommy-loving, forty-two-year-old-virgin haircut and jeans that nearly touched his nipples.

I almost did—strangle him that is. My phone buzzed just in time to save the poor man's life. Warren's small words of wisdom and encouragement were enough to distract me completely, if only for a few precious seconds.

Here now, where u?

I nearly leaped out of my skin as Joel finally began to meander away; he was always dead set on annoying just about anyone he could get close to in as little time as physically possible.

In back save me please!

I ignored the amused looks of onlookers as I tapped the keyboard as furiously as my fingers allowed, almost missing the send button in my haste. I was sure that at any moment the dragon otherwise known as Joel would return, if only to flay me alive.

My phone buzzed against the plastic tabletop:

Coming don't leave Need hugs and stuff.

I stayed put, my eyes scanning the adjacent hallway for any signs of trouble, ready to run if necessary.

Warren appeared before I had to run, sweeping in next to me like a white knight with a thick, curly black beard. He smiled as he cupped my face in his hands, kissing my nose and whispering hello.

I could almost feel the resentment filling the room.

Rebecca's sly glance met mine as she pushed herself past our mostly empty table. She chose to stake her claim on one of the few empty seats left behind us as truck unloaders began to swarm in, one after the other.

The smell of body odor and overused cologne mixed with leftover alcohol filled the room as tales of much older women and few and far between one-night stands began to buzz effortlessly in the air around my head.

Rebecca seemed undeterred, nowhere close to as repulsed as she probably should have been. Warren aside, these guys weren't exactly bring-home-to-Mother types. These were the kind of guys that left you alone and probably naked in the middle of the night.

No one besides myself seemed to notice as Joel continued to stand obliviously in the middle, like a child suddenly stuck in the earshot of adults.

Rebecca's chest was becoming the main display as Warren's attention remained focused on me, much to her dismay.

Her chest stuck out against a thin black T-shirt as she spoke.

Her eyes and lips puckered with pleasure as she took in her surroundings.

A half dozen young men, Joel not included, were completely unaware of her hormonal mating call.

It took everything I had not to burst out laughing, but then, glancing at my phone, I realized I was well past late.

Warren's soft eyes pleaded as he followed me to the time clock.

Rebecca's minions pushed past us and toward Miss Medusa herself, with equally snakelike eyes.

Janelle and Jessica wasted little time in joining Ms. My-shit-don't-stink as she did her best to snatch up whatever bait was available and/or willing, if not both.

These boys were so far from men it was truly hysterical to watch their attempts at swag as they sashayed toward receiving, at the far back corner of the store, where delivery trucks usually ended up. Blue jeans hung far below the knees, with belts that remained stuck hanging low against dimple-covered hips.

Kissing Warren good-bye, I sighed before making my way back up front, praying that the madness had neared its end.

Tommy's voice echoed over the intercom, calling for my speed and attention immediately.

I rolled my eyes.

I made it to my till before he could get truly riled up, pale eyes meeting mine over a rack of magazines.

My glare was more than able to outlast his, followed closely by a smile and smirk. Our friendship was much more work than the most complicated of relationships.

It was almost five thirty by the time Evelyn dared to bother me again. Her piercing green eyes caught a glimpse of my cell phone even from four tills away.

She rushed over to me just in time to catch a glimpse of what was so important that it had managed to take precedence over the group of middle-aged overly blonde women barking and bitching about a dollar-fifty price difference.

It was Warren, of course.

His dark eyes lit up my screen as he took one ridiculous picture of himself after another, his nose bunched up as he continued to chug a bottle of Frank's Hot Sauce.

"No phones on the sales floor; no phones on the sales floor," Evelyn whined, like a fire alarm decades out of practice and without a simple off switch.

"Thanks for the tip," I sneered, placing my phone facedown beside the printer, daring her to reach for it, to test whether or not she would still have fingers.

She didn't—test it, I mean.

Her long nose jutted into the air as she stalked away toward the podium where our so-called customer service managers stood gossiping and gallivanting as they shared an open box of sour gummy worms.

An assortment of black and white blackberries were displayed openly and obviously across the podium, large stacks of white receipt paper teetering destructively this way and that.

It took everything I had in me not to laugh, glancing over my shoulder one last time as Evelyn stormed back to her till.

Her dark curls bounced angrily up and down, and her furious eyes met mine one last time.

The words *this isn't over* were almost tangible in the frosty air that hung between us.

I somehow managed to make it through the rest of my shift mostly unscathed.

Warren's warm hands found mine as I pushed my way past the time clock. His lips touched my skin.

It was sad how easily I suddenly longed to stay, his presence the one and only thing able to keep me sane.

Ignoring the catcalls that filled the break room, his lips once again found mine.

"Where you going?" he asked, although I was sure that he already knew the answer, a fact that didn't seem to matter as his dark eyes met mine, pleading with me not to go anywhere.

"Home." I laughed as his hands found my back. "I have school tomorrow unfortunately, so I need to get home and sleep and do all that homework I haven't started yet."

He laughed, smiling at me as he leaned in. The fact that the school I was referring to carried the word *high* in front never seemed to faze him.

Our age difference once again shoved face-first out into the open. The five-year head start he had on life wasn't much. It was, however, enough for my seventeen-year-old ass to easily land his twenty-one-year-old ass in hot water should the unthinkable happen, of course.

The unthinkable was so thinkable that it was driving me insane. The thought of his lips on my skin was more than enough to distract me completely.

But my age or lack thereof wasn't the *only* reason our relationship had as of yet been unable to progress past the simple make-out stage, despite what everyone else around us may have been thinking, unable to be convinced otherwise.

I wasn't ready, a fact Warren knew and understood without judgment or pushing.

My knowledge of the facts of life was far too accurate for me to take that leap with someone that I barely knew; I had to know him inside and out, all the way through.

No horror movie would be able to withstand the true terror that the first morning after was sure to bring. My birthday suit was currently only available for my personal viewing.

Little aside from naked thoughts filled my head as I kissed Warren good-bye one last time before grabbing my jacket and making my way up front and out.

Where my mom sat patiently and waited, with a book pulled closely against her nose.

The van was toasty warm as I jumped in. Our conversation was limited to "How was your day?" and "I brought you Wendy's if you want it."

All the while our conversation left out the word that mattered most of all.

The word that changed all the rest.

The word I dared not speak for fear of a very awkward topic sentence and even more humiliating conclusion.

Instead, I shoved my face full of salty goodness as she drove along the snow-covered streets. I paused only long enough to take a sip of my pop, scared that if I choked, it would only draw more attention to the thoughts I was desperate to avoid.

"Where's Angie?" I asked finally, desperate to fill the silence that continued to lay between us as we reached the bridge that led straight to our house near the top of the hill.

"Somewhere with Luke, I would imagine." She shrugged, the topic of my sister not enough to dissolve whatever awkward air continued to linger between us, no matter the true subject matter.

Which usually ended up being her latest boyfriend, also known as whatever guy she had managed to snag.

My sex appeal was much more than lacking in comparison with that of my sister, who at five foot ten, with legs at least half that length, stood out among a sea of normal Riverside teenagers.

Most such teenagers had yet to graduate past the hoodie and blue jeans phase, not unlike myself.

My sister on the other hand?

Well, let's just say that when it came to her fashion sense, discount duds just weren't going to cut it.

No one else was home when we pulled up, so frenzied barking greeted us the second my feet hit the sidewalk.

Two furry faces poked out from between the curtains, tails wagging relentlessly, as if this alone would make us walk faster.

Ruffles and Cinnamon rushed toward us the second my mom's keys left the door. These two small white fur balls could never be defined by the word *dog*.

They were teddy bears, two slobbering welcome mats ready and much more than willing to lick you to death if necessary.

My phone clattered to the floor as they charged, tongue and tails armed and at the ready, innocent eyes glued to mine.

It was almost seven by the time I finally managed to escape to my cave.

The promise of food was more than enough to lure me back upstairs less than an hour later. The smell of potato chips filled the air as my mom clicked through the TV channels.

"How to lose ten pounds in ten days while eating the food you love? We will tell you how!" a woman not much older than myself screamed with about as much enthusiasm as a Chihuahua being chased by a pit bull.

"Fatima sisters, take Toronto!"

"Enjoy the lap of luxury that you yourself will never be able to obtain, all while feeling horrible about yourself right from the comfort of your living room!"

My mom's brown eyes met mine as we split open another bag, settling it against the couch cushions.

"What next?" I asked.

She laughed, reaching for Cinnamon as he attempted to leap against her legs.

The TV flashed multicolored versions of the exact same thing back at us as she scrolled—plastic looking for prey.

"So, how's Warren?"

Her voice caught me off guard.

As we settled on a true crime story drama, Cinnamon's thoughts seemed to mirror my own as I glanced at my buzzing phone, the screen illuminated eerily against my dad's favorite chair.

Danger! Danger!

"He's good, I guess." I shrugged, keeping my expression as nonchalant as possible. "Didn't want to work tonight, but that's nothing new."

I knew all the while that any mention of Warren, no matter how casual, was sure to bring up questions that I had no possible answers to.

The words *boyfriend* and Warren in the same sentence, let alone the *same room*, was much more than enough to completely freak me out.

The word *boyfriend* never really appealed to me much at all, let alone when an actual, real, living, breathing boy was involved.

A living, breathing boy who had far achieved manhood before I myself had managed to achieve the end of high school.

I didn't want a boyfriend.

I wanted Warren.

It was a difference that I feared my mother, let alone anyone else for that matter, would never be able to understand.

Chapter 8

I had only just tucked myself in mere hours later when the sound of my father's footsteps sounded in the space above my head.

Angie was not far behind, heels scraping against the hardwood, high-pitched voice carrying through the air and down the stairs with ease.

The words *OhmyGod* and *Luke is such a jackass!* vibrated violently in the space above my head. Her boy toy's name was all it took to lose my attention completely.

I was more than able to outlast the night without knowing the drama of my elder sister's love life.

Tall tales would be more than ready to mix with my breakfast cereal.

My dad's calm voice quickly began to fade as his voice rose in muted anger.

"Go to bed, okay, Angie? Just go to bed. Your sister is trying to sleep. We can talk about this in the morning."

What exactly *this* was that he was referring to I had no clue; I could only assume that it had to do with the obvious: Angie and Luke.

Luke was the doe-eyed, sweater-vested teenage mutant my sister had fallen head over heels for in less than three point four seconds.

Not that he was a bad guy or anything, although his communication skills left much to be desired. His mouth was rarely able to form words that didn't end in *ummm* or *okay uh thanks uh,* while my frustration boiled dangerously at the seams.

My nails were clenched against my skin as I nodded and smiled and played the perfect part of polite little sis. Words like *astronomical* and *extraterrestrial* bounced from one ear to the other and lingered in the space above my head.

You get my drift.

Frustrated cries brought me back to reality as Angie came barreling down the stairs toward my bedroom door. Her own makeshift cave was located only steps away, nestled in the far corner of my parents' basement.

In her cave, pinks mixed with pastels, and a curling iron was placed gently next to eyelash curlers more suitable for a street fight than to beautify one's face.

The edges of her frustration, like the edges of a flame, licked at my skin.

The door was cracked open just enough for me to get a full frontal view of the assault on her closet. Untouched clothes were tossed this way and that, and yoga pants were yanked high on her perfect size two unblemished waist.

I gave up.

That was enough.

I forced my eyes to the lines of my ceiling and shut my ears off to the world around me.

My phone was silent next to my bed, the clock counting down the last few seconds of Warren's shift.

I fell asleep soon thereafter, missing Warren's sweet good-bye and goodnight, which fired like a cannon in the city of the deaf. The glow of his name illuminated my walls in a sweet cobalt glow that went completely unseen, by me anyway.

My sister's eyes were not nearly as distracted as I would have liked. She had somehow still managed to read through feigned tears. Her screeching caught me completely off guard countless hours later.

I had only just hopped into the shower when her shrieks sent me nearly teetering over the side of the tub.

I had no idea what time it was.

My own balance leaving much to be desired as I rubbed what little sleep was left out of my eyes. A vicious voice echoed off the bathroom walls before I had even managed to wash, rinse, and repeat.

The morning had come much faster than I would have liked, and I was barely able to snatch my phone out of her greedy little hands before a look of true disdain filled her eyes.

It was disdain for anyone able to obtain that which she herself coveted most of all.

"So?" she asked as I reached for a towel, my wet feet slipping against the tile as I staggered my way toward my bedroom.

My tank top and shorts were still piled on the floor where I had stripped only minutes before.

Eager to avoid any and all forms of eye contact as she squealed, her accusations burned into my skin.

"I thought you said this guy wasn't your boyfriend, Emerson. After all, isn't that what you've been going around telling Mom?"

I almost choked.

Reaching for my hairbrush before allowing one quick glare to shoot into her eyes from mine, my cheeks felt suddenly red and hot, and my stomach started tying itself into knots.

"He's not, okay?" I choked out, my voice breaking in my attempt to appear little less than fearless.

Her eyes said everything, so she herself had no need at all to actually say, "Oh, really?"

"Do *non-boyfriends* text things like *good night, I guess, missing you and stuff?*"

Angie almost gagged.

She said the words with such flat disgust it almost made me cringe.

She followed me as I attempted to retreat, perfectly pressed nails holding my phone just far enough out of reach to fully earn the words I spat out next.

"Why?" I asked, pulling on an old pink T-shirt and my favorite brown sweatpants. "Does *Luke* never say anything like that?"

That was it. I had done it.

Unable to contain her fury, she stormed up the stairs and away from me, leaving my phone facedown on the pink-carpeted floor, vibrating silently.

Alyssa's good-morning message was left for the floor to read as I reached for my purse and whatever jacket I was able to grasp. I settled on a soft black number that Angie had left out during her rampage the night prior, not noticing the little pink-heart details until it was far too late.

Oh yes, today was going to be a *great* day.

I made it upstairs in record time, tucking my hair back behind my ears, my cheeks once against concealed in haphazard waves.

The benefits of refusing a haircut since age fifteen once again paid off in waves: there was no better way to conceal reddened acne-prone cheeks.

The front door stood teetering against the wall, as if retreating from Angie's dangerous fury. Her small red beater left little but a trail of black smoke in its wake, the tires revving against snow-covered pavement. She was gone before I even had the chance to flip her off, long brown hair blowing freely through the open window.

As if she couldn't get away from me fast enough, away from what I had said and the truth that lay behind it.

After all, it wasn't like we weren't going to see each other in five minutes or anything like that; we went to the exact same school for crying out loud.

I made it to the bus stop in record time, still able to taste the bitter smoke left behind by my ride.

Angie's icy glare seemed to follow me with the wind, easily burning holes through my thin yet fuzzy sweater, despite the fact that there was now and would forever be much more than simple distance that lingered between us.

Riverside High is located a few steps from downtown, the center of Riverside itself.

The small town of Riverside, in which Angie and I had grown up, nestled a safe and even distance between much larger and much more active cities and towns, where the words *break* and *enter* were much more than an adjective or a verb.

The bus was already packed with students much more miscreant than me, myself, and I, with baggy pants and eyebrows piercings that stood out against pale snow-stained skin.

Pale and freezing.

I narrowly avoided taking a backpack to the face while making my way toward the back and throwing myself down into the first empty seat that my ass came in contact with.

My phone was clutched tight in the palm of my hand. Warren's words burned white-hot inside my mind, etched against my skin.

Home now, u good and all? Missed you all night. Hate not being able to see you, need be here now.

It took everything I had not to smile like a complete idiot, and even more to stop once I had started.

The bus jerked to a stop as we reached the yellow-tinted curb. Baseball caps and backpacks filled the space above and around my head as everyone began to pile toward the exits.

Neon letters flashed violently against the fresh light of yet another snow-covered day: Riverside High, the true bane of my existence.

The faded red doors were far less than welcoming; the gray walls were almost black against the snow, and the windows were caked in mud and grease.

Here we go.

Taking as deep a breath as possible, I forced myself inside, legs heavy against the cement.

I didn't want to do this.

I didn't want to face what I knew I surely would face the second my hands were free of the cold steel that barricaded us inside. It cut off any and all chance of escape or free will, the lack of fresh oxygen affecting any and all brain cells.

My mind was unable to recall a time when just the thought of this place hadn't filled with me with fear and terror, terror of just what would happen next, fear of what I would do when it happened.

When the words of a girl not much different than myself left me splayed on the concrete.

Laughter vicious in the air.

My face was red with tears; I was open to humiliation and pain.

Eyes much crueler than any others I had ever seen mocked me from across the way, her voice unrelenting as she spoke, leaving me bruised and bleeding. Her words were more than able to break my bones, sticks and stones be damned.

I made it down the long hall that led to my locker just in time for the final warning bell to ring. Dozens of sneaker-clad feet were scattering every which way.

I was left alone and immobile, book bag clutched close against my chest.

I was waiting for the next strike of the gavel, the next chance for revenge.

I knew full well that the girl's words held little weight in contrast with my own. Any snide remark was no different than the few choice words I myself had used time and time again.

The town of Riverside divided when it came time for my extracurricular activities.

Teen writer accused of attacking classmates and hanging tormenters out to dry, the headlines had screamed. Time and time again, the parents of the leaders of my lynch mob never ceased in their self-appointed positions of judge, jury, and executioner. They convicted me on hearsay alone, any and all evidence tainted with tears and blood.

As if in the end I was just as bad as them, the people who held me as the definition of what was truly wrong with this school.

I was different.

I refused to give in.

Not now.

Not again.

That fact alone made me guiltier than anything else when people were faced with something they didn't understand.

And they did not understand someone who refused to give in, refused to pretend to be just like everyone else. Refused to stand on the sidelines while an angry mob of supporters ripped everyone else to shreds.

Well, let's just say, it only took the jury precious seconds to convict.

Chapter 9

I never saw her until I sat down.

Her wavy blonde hair was tinted gold in the fading sunlight. Her blue eyes avoided mine.

She was the girl who had tormented me, time and time again. The girl who had *enjoyed* it now sat silent.

The hunter was now the hunted, beaten down and weak.

My chest tightened as I realized once again just who it was that had done the beating.

Her delicate shoulders heaved as I took my seat, perfectly curled blonde hair concealing her unblemished face in waves.

Concealing each and every thought from me, the girl whose pain she had caused so easily.

Her words burned scars into my skin, cutting at my ribs.

"Ms. Winters, what a pleasure it is to have you finally join us," Mr. Williams cut in, pulling me away from my thoughts, distracting my eyes away from Maria, her cold eyes turned away from mine.

"Pages one to fifteen, come on, you heard me, come on. Open your books and at least pretend to pay attention."

His voice was stern, much sterner than the pale green eyes that stared back at the pupils seated unevenly in front of him.

Beakers and test tubes crowded along the counters, day-old experiments reminding those of us at least pretending to pay attention of what exactly it was that was in store for us during this ghastly hour: worm dissections.

I felt my stomach grumble and sweat dampen my forehead as Mr. Williams's voice bounced against the ceiling tiles.

"Pick a partner. Come on, people, not tomorrow or the next day, preferably right now. I don't care if it's your best friend or your ex-boyfriend! Wake up. It's Monday morning, for crying out loud! Wake up and get excited. This is science class, not nap time."

I didn't move.

Instead, I watched the trail of students leading precariously away from me, blondes avoiding brunettes.

Nerds headed toward the front of the class, any and all partnered groups refusing to be even slightly un-clichéd.

This was normal; this was expected.

Puzzle pieces that knew the best places to be positioned, while I sat silently, the odd girl out, the piece of the puzzle that just didn't fit.

Not even a little.

Not even a bit.

Not even at all.

"Emerson, you're with Maria," Mr. Williams announced, having noticed that I hadn't even attempted a partnering.

"Sean, you and Lincoln, center stage. Come on, people, let's get with this," he ordered, pale eyes meeting mine, unforgiving and unwilling to negotiate.

So I stood, feet heavy against the gray-painted concrete, forcing my eyes toward her face.

Pale skin unmoving, "Your desk or mine?" I called, all attempts at humor lost on such a poor defenseless soul, small shoulders rising ever so slightly.

Guilt radiated in my veins, guilt for causing the suffering of a girl to whom my own suffering had never been enough to earn a sideways glance as I barricaded myself in the bathroom time and time again, desperate and afraid.

"Fine. Your desk then, I guess," I mumbled, and pulled my desk alongside me, the legs screeching in protest.

I dropped my textbook an inch from her perfect flawless face, daring her to respond, to even roll her eyes.

Mr. Williams's chest heaved with impatience as he placed small metal containers evenly in front of us, not seeming to care what order it was that he placed them in.

The small helpless worms crawled uselessly toward freedom and escape, desperate for their lives, but they were unable to escape the grasp of some of my oxygen-deprived classmates.

Uncontrollable laughter penetrated the small helpless creatures as sharpened knives cut this way and that.

My own hand was tight against the small X-Acto knife when Maria's blue eyes met mine. "You first." I shrugged.

As I tried to force the small knife on her with no success, it was amazing to watch how easily she squealed, seat pulled so far away from mine I almost had to yell to be heard.

I was unable to tear my eyes away from the group of Maria look-alikes that had placed themselves perfectly in the corner. They were only steps away, able to hear every word, waiting for the slightest of signals, ready and willing to defend their master.

They had never realized, not even for the slightest of seconds, that maybe, just maybe, she wasn't the one who needed to be defended.

The clock struck nine before the small worm had even had the chance to negotiate, his long body flopping helplessly.

My hands were dried and bloody as I dropped the knife against the granite countertop for Mr. Williams to retrieve.

I ignored Maria's impatient sighs.

The room quickly emptied as students rushed this way and that, eager to get to their next class.

Maria's small frame shoved against mine with what I'm sure was all the force she could manage, sending my textbook flailing helplessly toward the cold and solid ground.

"Thanks," I called, not knowing if she was still within hearing and not caring regardless. "Don't worry about it. I'll get it no problem. Yeah, no problem whatsoever."

Laughter weighed against my bones, forcing my eyes to the ground as I pushed my way past them, ignoring the sideways glances and grunts, while words like *fat ass* floated in the air between us.

I winced as I felt my bag smash against my hip, the edges of a binder jabbing painfully into my skin.

I barely made it to the bathroom before my phone was out, fingers typing frantically.

I knew Warren was asleep, but I needed him regardless, suddenly desperate for the memory of his skin, warm against mine.

I wanted more than anything not to be Emerson Winters, tormented and now the tormenter. Infamous teen columnist, the girl apparently so at ease with hanging her enemies out to dry. Defenseless and unarmed, bruised and bleeding for the entire world to see. Week by week, day by day.

Instead, I wanted only to be Emerson, just Emerson, the girl Warren seemed to see every time his dark eyes stared back at me, gaze unyielding.

My thoughts were as incoherent as they ever were. Unable to stop myself, I typed a frantic and desperate plea:

Where are u?

It was almost noon by the time I felt my phone buzz again, a wakeup call against my skin.

I swiped my lock screen out of the way with much more force than was necessary and dropped myself against an empty bench.

Sleeping why what you did?

The breath of relief that flooded through me left me dizzy and lightheaded.

I didn't care what he was saying as long as I could read him saying it. As long as I wasn't alone, I could get through this. I *would* get through this.

Nothing, I typed, hitting send before continuing to type.

I was sure that this clingy side of me, so foreign against my skin, had already started to wear itself thin.

Just need you, I admitted, feeling utterly and completely pathetic.

I folded my bag against my lap, eyes scanning the hallway for any incoming attacks.

Should be here was all he said.

The words were much more tempting than I would ever be ready to admit.

I controlled myself long enough to respond with a quick and concise *I wish!*

I didn't notice Angie until it was far too late; suddenly I was engulfed with the smell of high heels and chiffon, plastic and unrelenting.

"Luke broke up with me!" she squealed as every fiber of my being silently screamed *I knew it!*

All the while I wished that her plea for companionship would be kind enough to fall on deaf ears. There was no part of me in a good enough mood to deal with this.

Not now.

Not today.

Not like this.

"He said we should see other people and that he wants back the promise ring I asked him to buy me for Valentine's Day!"

"Like really!"

She half squealed, half cried, "Who says that?"

I was sad to say that I kind of agreed.

Her shoes screeched against the floor as she dropped next to me with a bang, her gold-tinted purse sagging against her legs.

"I mean, what am I supposed to do?" she asked, looking to me for some sort of guidance, one hopeless cause needing another.

"We were supposed to go to the winter formal together, and now I have to go alone!"

Tears welled up against her eyelashes, smudging her perfectly applied eyeliner and sending trails of black smudge toward quivering, overglossed lips.

"I mean, what am I supposed to do without him? He's the only decent boyfriend I've ever had! Even Andrew wasn't as nice as Luke was, and Andrew bought me the *cutest* Oakley sunglasses for Christmas the year before last."

I chuckled recalling one of the finer species of male to be pulled into my sister's web of dating destruction.

Tall and elite, Andrew had blue eyes that had crinkled with amusement as they met mine, as overly used jokes never failed to escape his thin prissy lips.

His soft voice was full of laughter as he witnessed what my parents and I had been forced to live with, indifferent to the hysterics forced on us by decades of genetics.

It all pooled into one five-foot-ten doe-eyed teenage it girl, parading happily for all of Riverside to see.

"Come on," she had pouted, bright eyes glowing against the darkening sky, smile widening against the night.

Andrew was helpless in her presence, just like every other man aside from our father. Andrew was a man bound by respect and proper behavior, and his tired blue eyes met mine with tired amusement.

"Please?" she begged and pleaded.

She knew full well that she always got her way, one way or another, and in the end, that was all that mattered to her.

"Look, baby, I would love to be able to take all of my classes with you this semester, but I just can't, okay? I'm sorry, but I've got to get my grades up. There's no way that U of A will look at me otherwise."

Andrew shrugged as Angie grumbled, the voice of reason lost on her completely, as if Andrew were speaking to a brick wall or an empty garbage can.

"What am I going to do?" Angie cried, yanking me from my memories and splashing her unreasonable grief smack-dab into my face.

"I mean, Luke was only my third *real* boyfriend, which means my third *real* kiss, you know, without all that other stuff."

Her face scrunched up as she spoke, words rubbing together like sandpaper, their meaning completely lost on me. The snow-tainted sun streaming through the dirty splattered window with ease illuminated her face.

The hallway was silent apart from the varied chattering, third period long since having started. I wondered vaguely if anyone had taken the time to notice that I hadn't arrived yet.

"Third *real* kiss?" I asked, flabbergasted. "What is that? Some kind of code word for French kissing?"

My mind retraced the steps Warren had taken between my lips and his, time and time again.

My first time was so at odds with how Angie described it, heated and unleashed, laughter erupting from his chest with ease, strong hands clumsy against mine. It was months ago the first time that it had happened.

It was the first time that I had given in, young and still as inexperienced as a child just learning how to take his or her first steps, guided slowly by a parent far too protective to ever risk losing his or her grip.

"What?" Warren had laughed, holding the pool cue lightly against my hip, taking readied stance against the table.

Lights, camera, action.

My own grip slipped ever so slightly, just enough to send the both of us flailing forward, our chins grinding against the carpeted edges of the pool table, dusty from time spent unused, standing guard center stage in the middle of his parents' downstairs living room.

"Oh my God!" I yelped, hands jutting out in defense, pool cue flailing upward, hitting its mark right on target and with all the force that a teenage girl could manage.

Warren's own grunts and groans were enough to send me fleeing for safety, hiding against the washing machine, as he held his junk protectively, for only my eyes to see.

"Oh my God, I am so sorry!" I screamed, sure that this was it, that I had done it, once and for all, no going back.

After all, how many relationships have you heard of that can survive a direct unprecedented shot to the junk? With a pool cue of all choice of weapons, tongs and shovels included.

"Are you okay?" I cried, words falling on deaf ears.

His moans were sure to wake his parents at one point or another.

He nodded, dark eyes wide open and full of pain only another male could comprehend.

Kiss me, he mouthed, barely managing to wave me forward, hands still clutched tightly against his abdomen.

I didn't move.

I was sure that any step toward him would only result in further humiliation and misery. Pain inflicted from one klutz to anyone and everyone that dared stand too close.

Kiss me, he mouthed again. Then Warren smiled, laughing slightly, daring me to move and daring me to trust him, just this once.

Just like that.

"Kiss me?" he asked again, so I did.

Chapter 10

The cafeteria was packed by the time I finally managed to pull myself out of Angie's tear-dampened grasp.

Large plastic tables were divided by cliques. The popular crowd took center stage, while the rest of us teenage delinquents settled in among ourselves.

"Hey hey." Kassie smiled, planting herself next to me.

Her dark hair was frizzy and haphazard. Her teal-painted eyes scanned the room for any sign of meat worthy enough to glance at.

The search ended with the words that silenced all the rest, words that hung heavily in the warmth that lingered between us. "So, where is Warren anyway?" she teased, giggling slightly as she elbowed me, beige skin glowing against the fluorescent lighting.

It was hard to remember a time when we hadn't been friends.

The queen bee wannabe and the disinterested, like lukewarm water mixed with tar.

We fit, though, oddly enough.

"Warren?" I shot back, aghast. "Now, who might that be? Sounds like a fine gentleman if you ask me."

Kassie laughed, the sound soft and gentle against a wall of noise bashing violently against my brain.

Distracted as I dropped my bag against her legs, I made my way toward the line that had started to resemble a mosh pit. Hungry students were all intent on leaving with a plate of Riverside's best French fries—curly and delicious.

I didn't see her until it was far too late. It only took mere moments for her eyes to meet mine, ice-cold and snakelike.

Smirk indented against porcelain skin, unrelenting as her glance bore past me.

All the while I didn't know what it was that she was truly glaring at—Kassie perhaps?

Anyone who had ever dared to stand against her, my best friend included, was enough to ignite Rebecca's scathing rage.

I shrugged it off, knowing that there was nothing I could do regardless.

I held my wallet tight against my palm as she passed slowly by me.

Don't let her get to you, I silently pleaded.

I am allowed to eat, I reminded myself scathingly.

I am allowed to be here.

I am allowed to breathe.

Rebecca's shoulder hit mine with all the subtlety of a rock slide, covering my face with ash and burying me alive.

"Please move," I mumbled, my nerves getting the better of me, the taste of acid burning my throat and leaving scars blatant and burning, wide-awake and flaming.

"Why?" she asked. "Not enough room here for the both of us? You know I never did understand how Warren managed to get his hands around those gigantic hips."

It took everything I had in me not to lunge, not to scratch her eyes out and redden the skin around her throat.

Why oh why did there have to be only *one* school district in all of Riverside?

One prison. The gates of hell welcoming me with ease, surrounding me with smiles and frowns too uncertain to be believed.

"Actually, Rebecca, Warren has never had a problem wrapping his arms around me."

I smiled. My next words were enough to send the both of us reeling, undaunted and unbelieving.

"Which is more than I can say for anyone left with the daunting task of wrapping his or her arms around *you*."

Even as I walked away, I felt bad.

Kassie's teal eyes met mine with ease as she slid across the bench to make room for my fries, my attitude problem, and me.

My bag once again hit the ground with a thud as my mind raged, *She deserved it!*

The words banged around my brain like a hammer searching for a nail, violent and unrelenting.

"You know Warren would never go for her, right?" Kassie tried, sighing as her pity weighed against me.

Rebecca was now miles away, the crowd coming together, blending in the space they had vacated to allow her escape.

"He loves you. Girls like that mean nothing to him. I mean, even I can see that!"

"Girls like that?" I laughed, the sound weak and pathetic. "You mean girls that tear each other down just to make themselves feel better?"

"Well, yeah," she sighed, never seeming to realize, even for a fraction of a second, that one of those girls, so full of misery and conceit, was sitting right next to her.

Chapter 11

I don't know how I made it through my next two classes without throwing up. My mouth and tongue were bitter with the effort, the grinding of my teeth.

I had let Rebecca get to me, once again, just like she had wanted, just like I knew she would. The words that escaped her lips so easily cut like knives against me, burying me with clay.

I wanted to hurt her. I wanted to run away. I wanted to cry without the fury of letting her get her way—her sick, twisted way.

"Warren loves you." Kassie had shrugged so easily, the words falling flat against unbending fury.

I love him was the only thing that I could think, never letting myself believe, even for a fraction of a second, that there was any chance that *he* could truly love *me*.

It was still snowing by the time I finally managed to push my way outside, the concrete ground dusted with mud and snowflakes, escape no longer so distant and fleeting.

I wanted to run.

I needed to run.

I needed to get away.

I needed to push the thoughts of this place so far deep down within me that they would curl against my stomach, burning against my skin, leaving every inch of me damaged and scarred, my insides bruised and bleeding.

My feet moved faster than even my mind could comprehend as I rushed toward the only empty bus stop. I was sure that if I only just moved that much faster, the taunting would never have a chance to touch me.

Words that stung like ice chips in the sand sliced against already dry and aching skin, echoing against the winter's wind, not so friendly ghosts of a moment long since past.

A blonde girl so much younger than I was now stood alone and freezing, brown eyes dusted with tears too rigid to ever brush her cheeks.

"Em, wait!"

Kassie's voice struck me like a brick, yanking me back toward her from the edge.

The small blonde girl's neck snapped quickly this way and that, her expression vanishing with the wind as easily as if it were sand.

"Hey, what's up? Are you okay? You looked like you were kind of lost for a second back there. What's going on? Is this about Rebecca? What she said about Warren?"

"No." I lied, unable to tear my eyes away from the ground, so cold and hollow. "I'm fine. I just really need to get home is all; my mom needs me for some sewing project."

My lie wasn't that far off base.

Not really.

All anyone had to do was notice how easily my pants dragged along the sodden ground to realize that maybe, just maybe, I should be introduced to some slight hemming.

Kassie just stared, as if attempting to penetrate whatever wall it was that I had started to build there. Concrete mixed with brick.

I was sure that there was no better way to protect myself than this, to block out all the voices that threatened to overtake me completely, memories that could shatter glass.

Instead, "Want a ride?" was all she said, smiling lightly as she linked her arm against mine. I merely nodded, forcing myself to breathe deeply as I allowed the cold dampness of the snow to touch me washing clean against my skin, leaving me shiny and new, as if somehow, by some miracle, it was truly possible to start fresh and new.

No one was home but Angie, of course.

Her small red Mustang was parked just where it always was, blocking both the sidewalk and the driveway.

"You sure you wouldn't just rather come hang at my place instead?" Kassie asked as innocently as possible, for what must have been the four hundredth time since she hit unlock and turned the key on the old blue Sentra her parents had gifted her for her eighteenth birthday.

"I mean, your mom probably isn't going to get home for another hour, right? To do the whole sewing thing? I can always bring you back later, after we get food or whatnot." She shrugged, eyeing me helplessly.

Kassie was the only other person in the universe capable of dreading Angie's company as much, if not more so, than yours truly. But she was so willing and ready to put herself in harm's way for me if necessary.

"It's okay." I laughed, sparing her the carnage and cat claws as I hopped onto the curb, unable to shake the idiotic part of me so unable to let people in.

Everyone except Warren.

My mind was not molded with the idea of spending time with people my own age, often, in public. I just wasn't built that way.

Even with Kassie, the one girl I had been closer to than any other I had been cursed to spend my school years with. Even with Kassie, I still didn't quite fit.

I never quite knew what to say or how to act, our friendship barely existing outside the Riverside High hallways. Despite Kassie's continued attempts, I wouldn't have known what to say regardless.

There was just this. The halls of Riverside high, now empty and silent.

Our friendship was just that.

My mind distracted, I narrowly avoided landing face-first against the curb. My eyes caught only the briefest glance of the fresh snow and ice that dusted the ground beneath my feet.

It was a death trap just waiting for the right person distracted and dizzy enough to step right into its painful grasp.

Angie wasn't upstairs when I got in, but the TV was blaring much louder than necessary. Jerry Springer was doing his best to appear genuinely concerned over which saggy-pants, bandana-wearing stud truly was the father.

I'm sad to say that I actually caught myself caring too as I stripped off what a day of torture had left behind: sodden socks and pants dampened up to the knees, my hair now a tangled mess that didn't even start to unravel until well past my cheeks.

The dogs were more than happy to park themselves in front of me as I slipped into my favorite pair of pajama pants and made myself at home on the couch, a warm bowl of popcorn settled comfortably against my legs.

It wasn't until at least an hour later that I felt my phone buzzing as Angie finally sucked it up and started to make her way upstairs.

It was Warren, of course.

He was only an hour deep into his shift and already wanting to leave and wanting to see me, whichever was more possible and could happen as soon as possible.

Joel? I asked, unable to type with the minimum amount of surprise and amusement possible.

Who else? he shot back, faster than I even thought possible, his hands already clicking against the screen before my reply was even ready, hands far less furious than his.

Swear to fuck this guy has zero brain cells! Just standing there all derping out staring at boxes like he expecting them to get up and start moving themselves around!

Just wanna scream at him seriously DO SOMETHING FOR FUCKS SAKE!

I laughed just in time for Angie to *finally* get upstairs, dragging her feet much more than necessary.

She was pouting enough to give herself one of those overly used and overly expensive, overly plumped looks that all the girls like her seem to be vying so desperately for.

"What?" she sneered, plopping down dramatically next to me as both Ruffles and Cinnamon jumped up to run for cover, tails wagging furiously behind them.

I forced myself to bite my tongue. I fought the urge to yell out, *Was I talking to you? I don't think so!*

Instead, settling back against the couch cushions as I shrugged, I placed my phone's screen flat against my lap.

I was sure that at any moment she was sure to reach for it, perfectly manicured nails tapping nervously against her palms.

Her voice was low and unsteady as she asked, "Why doesn't he want me anymore? What did I do wrong?"

I froze in shock, unsure of what to say or do. I was too uncomfortable to move as Jerry continued to banter with a woman more than twice his age and size, blonde cornrows ending messily against the back of her legs.

"I'm sorry." I shrugged, honesty pulling at my insides. "I'm sorry, I don't … I mean, are you sure he doesn't *really* want you? Did he say or did you ask … ?"

My voice trailed off as Angie pulled away from me with disgust, her expression quickly changing from shock to outright disbelief that I could ever suggest such a thing.

"You don't *ask* a guy that, Emerson! What is wrong with you? Oh my God!"

She was up and enraged before I could do anything about it, already a million miles out of my reach.

"I bet this is all about that stupid Suzie in his gym class. She's constantly walking around in leggings *right in front of my boyfriend! My boyfriend!*"

Angie continued to squeal, a lost cause intent on destruction, perfectly applied eyeliner now smudged in an ugly pink line across her cheeks.

I was almost ashamed to admit that there was a part of me, however small and undiscoverable, that didn't exactly *disagree* with what my firecracker disaster of a sister was saying. Leggings as pants wasn't exactly the most alluring look on everyone, myself included.

Although I couldn't help but hope that Luke, of all people, overachieving suck-up that he was, would have had more of a brain than to spend his gym time ogling at girls in overly tight and jet-black track pants.

That's what free porn is for.

I didn't say any of this, of course, though I don't think Angie would have heard me anyway.

Her tirade was far from finished, perfectly manicured nails digging deep into her palms, perfectly made-up eyes bulging beyond measure.

The TV broke my concentration as Jerry's audience screamed with the kind of fever only found on scripted reality talk shows, *"Jerry, Jerry, Jerry!"*

One overly tanned woman grabbed at another as a row of oversize, underdressed, sure soon-to-be ex-husbands looked on with glee and pleasure.

"Emerson!" Angie screeched, voice unrelenting. "Are you even listening to me?"

Of course not.

"Yeah, I was just thinking about what you said." I lied, pulling my eyes away from the TV.

Three scantily dressed bimbos now fought for dominance in a pool full of red and green Jell-O.

The sound of my phone buzzing wildly against my palm signaled me just how late it was.

Warren's words glowed back at me in all of their blue-tinted glory.

The six little words erased anything anyone else had said or done throughout the entire afternoon. Angie was now no more than an irritating little fly on the windowsill.

I need to see you now

I don't know how I made it downstairs without giving anything away, my face flushed with the rush. I was sure that any second, Angie was bound to come barreling in behind me. Her hands would snatch freshly folded clothes out of my hands, surely able to read what must be written so obviously all over my face.

After all, this was it, wasn't it?

The feeling all those romance novels and PG-13 movies had spent all that time describing?

The moment when you just knew that *that* was what you needed to do?

The one moment, the one thing in the entire known universe that could leave you feeling warm, safe, and comforted?

This was it, wasn't it?

I could only hope as I pulled on whatever clothes my hands managed to grasp, that this need wasn't one that would dull with ease, his hands forever wrapped around me, warm, safe, and comforting.

Steadying me even when I couldn't steady myself, torturing me with his kind and easy smile. Sending shivers down my spine as he said, "I need to see you now."

There was only one thing I knew: I needed to see him too.

Chapter 12

I made it to Tagman's just before eleven.

Angie was much more willing to lend me her car than I thought she would have been, what with that whole against-the-law, not-really-licensed-yet, little tidbit—even though I probably could have driven circles around her, and then some.

The store was as crowded as ever, even though they had technically closed almost an hour earlier.

Shopping carts loaded with toddlers and ice cream bars poured in and out of the front doors, children screaming and crying, understandable since it was way beyond their bedtime, not that the parents seemed to care.

It was then that I saw him as I stayed put in one of the few free parking spots, Angie's engine sputtering the way you would expect from an aging and grumpy senior.

Warren.

He looked the same for the most part, of course. Long silky black hair ending in ringlet curls halfway down his back. Large brown eyes that stared never-endingly back into mine. A smile kinder and shier than any I had ever known.

Something was different, though, something that I just couldn't place.

Hands as soft as ever, he leaned over Angie's day-old coffee to kiss and tickle me, fingers clenched tightly against the back of my hand, the lines of his face heavy and exhausted.

"How was work?" I forced myself to ask, my voice much more chipper than necessary.

My nerves threatened to bubble over. "Goddamn, Joel is a useless fuck," Warren yelled in frustration, reaching across me and toward the window controls.

His voice was always on the edge of laughter where Joel was concerned. His patience when it came to the one guy everyone at Tagman's was determined to avoid was truly something to be admired.

His dark eyes full of amusement and awe as he spoke, the latest drama that Tagman's had produced was enough to keep him talking as I drove.

"What'd he do now?" I almost laughed, more than used to the antics of the one person with more commentary to add to our relationship than anyone else I had ever known.

"I'm pulling a skid of water by myself, of course, and stupid guy has to follow me all the way out of receiving waving his hands in the air, talking about some movie he went and saw with his mom over the weekend."

Joel, despite being forty-something pushing fifty, had as of yet been unable to graduate past the stage of living with his parents and having regular movie and dinner dates with his reclusive mother.

Warren's frustrations bounced off the windows and back at us as we drove, the streets silent and snow-covered.

The streetlights dimmed with the night sky, as if somehow preparing for sunrise.

My phone was completely silent in my lap. My mother's response to my spending the night at Kassie's was less than thrilled, the words "it's a school night" managing to escape her mouth at least once or twice.

The sky was now completely silent.

The sidewalk in front of Warren's building was dusted with snow and ice, his warm hand strong and steady against mine.

He never said a word as we made our way up the stairs, merely smiling as I narrowly avoided falling head-first ahead of him, my feet clumsy with nerves.

For what, I wasn't actually sure.

I had been in his place a million-plus times. The tan counter was still littered with Red Bulls and Pepsi bottles, and the couch appeared frozen and untouched.

The cushions were still indented with my touch, and the window sealed against the wind and snow.

Despite all this, I felt myself freaking out a little, unable to recall a time when I had been out until midnight.

At a boy's place, no less—a boy much more man than he was prepubescent.

My mother's dark brown eyes suddenly came alive and vivid in my mind, her voice unsure and high-pitched.

It was as if a part of her were standing there in front of me, instead of at home with my dad, her voice bouncing around inside my head, as if she were really asking, "Are you sure you want to do this?"

I wasn't actually.

No part of me was prepared for the moment Warren walked up slowly behind me.

He wrapped his arms around my waist and made me feel small and beautiful when he said, "I love you."

Every fiber of my being screamed with a need that no matter how hard I tried, I just couldn't understand.

My lips crashed into his with a feeling I couldn't comprehend, his hands against my face, my back. My skin was on fire against him. Our feet were tangled against the carpet, my chest pressed unyieldingly against his.

There was no pain in the world that could ever justify missing this, his lips at my neck.

Hands against my skin, pulling me against him, his voice sweet and breathless as we crashed against the sheets and pillows of a mismatched mattress, blankets like silk against my bare skin.

Never in my life had I felt safety like this.

My hands against his chest, lips against his neck—I don't know how long we stayed like that.

His back curled against my chest, hands clenched against him, our legs entwined and twisted.

He was mine, and I was his.

"You okay?" Warren whispered, his quiet voice like an echo in the darkness, guilt radiating in his veins.

I nodded, unable to find the words to explain what had just happened. The word *okay* just didn't seem to fit.

I pulled what sheets I could grasp against my chest, desperate for some kind of distance to be placed between us, even in the darkness.

My skin was on fire where it touched his. My hands traced circles against his chest, unable to distract myself from what had just happened.

"God, I love you," he whispered, so quietly I wasn't sure if it was meant for me or just himself to hear, lips eager against my hands as he pulled my legs tighter against his.

His hands at my waist, pulling me closer still until I was tied against him, lips against my skin.

Never in my life had I dreamed of a night like this.

I awoke countless hours later to the sound of sirens, impatient and squealing, one after another.

The sunrise lit up the sky as if it were on fire, clouds burning away from the flame that burned too hot to smother.

It was the first day in weeks that hadn't greeted us with snow and ice, rain chunks that fell heavily from the sky.

Feeling my face flush, I glanced at Warren, his pillows dented and wrinkled.

The sheets were tucked in and around him, his chest so close that I felt the need to back up a little.

"What?" He laughed, brushing the hair from my face as his lips once again touched mine, soft and restrained.

Laughter shook his chest as he groaned.

He seemed unable to keep his hands away from my face, my shoulders, any part of me that he could reach.

"My mom has probably been calling me for hours," I sighed, hating to ruin the moment.

I knew that the second I stood up, the sheets would drop against my legs. How easily the cold early morning air would hit me, leaving me defenseless, with nothing but the darkness to hide behind—and my own inhibitions.

"Just stay, please," Warren pleaded, refusing to let me go, not that there was any part of me that wanted him to. Not even a little, not even at all.

"I can't." I shrugged, my mind raging, *can't* or *don't want to?* Every fiber of my being longed to be right where I was now, safe, warm, and wanted.

My mother's eyes burned bright in the back of my mind, with torrid stories of first loves and first times gone awry.

"Boys are after one thing and one thing only, one thing that no matter how much you might want it to, can never be changed. Never, no how, no way."

Her eyes creased time and time again as she sighed, relating memories of a boy not much older than I was now, eager and familiar. It made sense. Even if the couple sometimes didn't.

"You can never change it," she had told me time and time again, eyes focused only on the road ahead.

"Your first time is everything. You can never change who it was with. If he's an asshole, well, too bad, because for the rest of your life, it's always going to be him. You'll never be able to change that."

Her voice seeming to echo in the darkness as my hand found Warren's, pressed gently against his chest.

"It changes you. For the rest of your life, whoever you're with, it's never going to be the same again. Whenever you're ready, whoever you decide is worth it better be in the end."

I don't know how we managed to untangle ourselves and get dressed.

My legs were suddenly more clumsy than they had been ever before. My palms were dampened with sweat and nerves. My hair, pushed back into a ponytail, stuck to my forehead with sweat no matter how many times I tried to unstick it.

"I don't want you to go."

Warren's voice caught me off guard, so quiet and full of a longing and a pain I couldn't understand.

At least not yet.

"I know, but I have to." I laughed, or at least attempted it, sure that whatever was waiting for me at home wouldn't be nearly as kind or understanding as what I had here.

More than happily borrowing one sister's car despite being totally and completely unlicensed to do so.

I couldn't imagine how *that* was going to go over, not to mention that the same seventeen-year-old unlicensed teenager lied about where she was going and stayed out until sunrise.

I couldn't wait to go home and hear what they were going to say about that!

"Good-bye, I guess." I laughed, reaching for my backpack and making my way toward the front door.

His hands caught me by surprise, pulling me against the kitchen wall and holding me there, safe and in place.

"I'll see you tomorrow," I promised, suddenly remembering that my shift at Tagman's that started at six sharp.

"That's like forever, though," he pouted, which for a six-foot-and-some truck unloader was actually pretty hilarious.

Any masculinity he had jumped out the window and ran away, not that I minded, and sadly enough, neither did he suddenly.

I laughed, reaching in my jacket pocket for Angie's car keys, sure that any moment some secret alarm she had installed was bound to start going off.

I didn't think that whole, "Sure, I'll lend you my car" thing had extended this far past midnight.

"I have to go," I urged, pulling regretfully away from him, the words *I love you* forming on my lips before I was able to do anything about it.

Warren never hesitated. His smile beamed louder than the sirens, amusement shaking his chest.

As the door shut slowly behind me, I had no idea how I had ever managed to leave him like that.

Chapter 13

It was full-on morning by the time I got home. My dad's truck was parked in the driveway. Somehow, right away, I just knew that I was in trouble.

His shift was not due to end for *at least* another three hours or so, sixteen hours spent on the road.

Monday through Thursday night wasn't exactly something that could be cut short just like that, not unless something major had happened.

And happen it had.

Leaving the Mustang doors open, I sauntered my way up the front steps, desperate to wipe any and all evidence of what had happened quickly and painlessly away.

The front door was unlocked and open just enough for me to get a peek inside. My mom heard me, of course. Probably before I had even set foot on the stairs, Angie's Mustang not exactly what *anyone* would call stealthy.

"Hey," I called, pushing my way past a long-forgotten laundry basket and toward my dad, who was sitting in his favorite chair reading the newspaper.

A plate of sausage and eggs was going stale on the living room table, teasing Ruffles and Cinnamon relentlessly.

"Hey, brat," he sighed tiredly, seemingly shocked by my sudden appearance, understandable considering I hadn't even been on this side of town during breakfast.

"Where the hell have you been?" my mother yelled.

I froze; I had been waiting for this.

My mom slammed the fridge shut with more force than necessary; I swear I heard the eggs teeter and fall against the bottom shelf.

"With Kassie." I lied as innocently as possible, playing shell-shocked and confused quite well. "Angie told me she would tell you guys what happened. Kassie's parents have been arguing and would not stop; she really needed me."

"Angie has been gone all damn night with Luke doing God knows what!"

My dad's voice bounded across the living room, blue eyes sad and tired.

"Oh," I said.

I felt my face redden, knowing just what that *God knows what* really was.

"I'm sorry. I didn't know where she was." I shrugged, desperate to escape this interrogation.

"Can I go now?" I called, already halfway down the stairs in my mind, sure that the longer I stood there, the more likely it was that I would appear guiltier and guiltier. "I really want to shower."

My mom nodded, sighing into her coffee cup, brown eyes barely glancing up from the counter as I booked my way downstairs, dropping my T-shirt and jeans to the floor without a very concentrated effort.

The water was like a breath of fresh air. It was the first time that I had really let myself breathe in hours.

Every muscle was tense and sore.

My hands rested easily against the cold tile wall, my neck seeming to relax with the water.

Had it only been an hour? An hour since I woke up with Warren curled against me, his back like a map, scars that told stories of this and that, strong arms wrapped forever around me, warm, safe, and comforting.

As if protecting me from some evil that as hard as I tried, I just couldn't see.

His voice was quiet and kind as he did his best not to hurt me, holding me as close as he dared, as if desperate to maintain a safe distance, as if he didn't know what he might do if I got too close.

It was a limit I didn't dare test, a line I'd rather not have crossed, my mind and body only able to handle so much.

His legs were soft and strong against mine, pulling me up and holding me still, swaying as gently as he was able.

"You're fine," he promised.

I couldn't doubt his honesty; it rang in every word.

"I love you, okay? You're fine, baby. You're fine; I got you."

"I love you too."

It was the first time I had ever said the words out loud, my eyes closing with the sound.

I swear I heard his heart stop just a little, hands gentle against my back as he lifted me from his lap, laying me gently against the mattress.

He always seemed to be guarding me from something, hands against my back, my body hungry as I pressed my lips against his.

"Be mine, baby," he breathed, voice against my neck, lips against my chest, the darkness seeming to swallow us as we moved, becoming one instead of two.

There was no part of my body that was not synced with his, every motion being mimicked in the darkness.

The world did not exist; there was only this.

"You okay in there?"

It was my mom, of course, shaking me from my reverie.

"Yeah," I sighed. "I'm fine." I shrugged, as if wondering what her problem was. Couldn't a girl just shower in peace for once in her life?

I was desperate for some semblance of alone time, my thoughts still a tangled and incoherent mess.

"Just checking," she mumbled quickly before closing the door and retreating the four steps to the laundry room.

My dad's coveralls needed to be taken out of the drier before they ended up fitting my Ken doll better than they fit him.

By the time I got to my bedroom and got dressed, there was only fifteen minutes until my science class started.

Angie's corner bedroom was still devoid of her perky overzealous presence.

Which meant there was one option and one option only that could result in me actually getting to school on time for maybe the first time in my life.

"Mom?" I hollered, dropping my bag against the bed, my phone still unmoving and silent.

I was still clutching it tightly against the palm of my hand as my mom hit the unlock button on the van minutes later, dropping her purse between our seats as we both jumped in.

The ride to Riverside High was a lot quieter than it could have been, the radio humming quietly as I stared at the early morning sky, willing the time to pass by.

"So, Kelsey called," my mom began. She smiled, eyeing me, the subtle giveaway that this was gong to be a very good story.

Kelsey, my forty-two-year-old-and-then-some aunt, wasn't exactly what anyone would call modest.

Ditzy, perhaps.

Modest?

Never, no way, not a chance.

"She called last night bawling that her butler never showed up; whined for a good half an hour while your dad and I were trying to make supper."

Kelsey, the woman of too much money and not enough time in the world to be spent whining about it.

Prada's not perky enough perhaps?

"I told her we're trying to eat, I'll call you later, okay? Oh no, she says, *you don't understand!*"

My mom continued, mimicking Kelsey's high-pitched and overly dramatic voice perfectly.

It never ceased to amaze me how a woman who shared *actual* DNA with a man who worked sixteen hours every day in order to make a living had wound up living in one of the most exclusive neighborhoods one could find in Riverside, while she spent most of her time complaining about it.

Her marriage to a wealthy web developer named Henry Something or other ended long before my thirteenth birthday after only starting not long before my eleventh.

The monthly hush money he was then forced to fork over at least twice a month due to his web-developing skin beginning and ending with the word Google, would have been much better spent at ending world hunger, or at least put toward buying himself a brand-new European sports car.

It was only when my mom started to laugh that I realized I had actually said all of that *out loud*.

My face flushed red.

"Oh well." She laughed, shrugging. "You know your dad's little sister."

Yes, yes, I did.

All too well actually.

We were at school by then, the rusted front doors just as uninviting and terrifying as they had been the day before. There was no welcome mat for me here, no kindness or safety or warmth.

My entire frame swayed back and forth as my feet touched the pavement, every fiber of my being longing to be the exact opposite of where I was now.

I was alone and filled with dread.

Memories of a safer place, my back pressed gently against Warren's headrest, burned against my skin. There was no place more opposite than that.

Chapter 14

Mr. Williams was already wide-awake and demanding by the time I actually made it to the science lab. Every desk was taken aside from the one next to Maria.

Never had a cliché been so true as it was right now. You would have thought I was some diseased, creepy-ass honcho by the way she scooted so quickly against the wall.

Every fiber of my being screamed at me not to as I dropped my bag to the floor, turning so that my eyes focused directly and scornfully on hers.

The words slipped out without my brain ever truly giving them permission to do so: "Stop, okay? Just stop!"

My voice came out not nearly as pleasantly, demanding her attention, and refusing to give in until I received all four precious seconds of it.

"What?" she asked, seemingly flabbergasted that anyone not as perfect as she apparently thought she was, would ever dare speak to her in such a manner.

"Stop acting like I'm just a rodent you can get away from. Just because I'm not a size minus two like you doesn't mean that I'm gross or stupid or useless or some ignorant fool.

"Do you have any idea of the past four years at all? Of all the crap that you put me through?"

The words exploded from my chest as from a rocket launcher, unrestrained and without a safety switch.

I was dead-set ready and aimed perfectly, her blue eyes staring terrified back into mine.

"You locked me in the bathroom, telling me that I'm so fat I should just go kill myself."

I was on a roll now, four years of pent-up emotions flowing freely and out of control.

"You tormented me, Maria, and for what? Where did it really get you in the end?

"When I was thirteen years old, I went to my best friend's sleepover—my best friend's!

"Of course, when I got up the stairs, you were there, laughing at me for being out of breath and telling everyone that I had greasy hair.

"When I went to the bathroom, you told everyone I wiped my ass with a facecloth, didn't you?

"You told everyone I was a gross and disgusting pig too stupid to even use toilet paper."

The room was silent now aside from my pounding heart and my voice strangled and strangely high-pitched.

"I spent every day being told how ugly I was by *you*. Every fucking day you would pass by me in the halls and wait for me to do something worth laughing about, wouldn't you?

"I'd pull up my pants, and you'd act like it was the funniest thing in the world.

"You'd wait until my acne would break out again and spend the entire class pointing at me and calling me Rudolph. I used to cake on makeup because of you!

"I couldn't even get myself to go to bed, for crying out loud, without making sure that every single red patch of my skin was covered by greasy tan-colored gunk.

"I could barely live with the way I looked, and still, here you are acting like none of that ever happened, like the things you do or say don't affect people.

"What the fuck is wrong with you?"

She laughed then, actually fucking laughed! As if completely oblivious to everything I had just said. As if my pain meant nothing to her, which of course it didn't.

"What the fuck is wrong with me?" Maria shouted, turning to face me head-on now.

"What the fuck is wrong with you, Emerson?

"I mean, seriously, crying because I called you ugly every day? Well, guess what? I was right; you *were* ugly.

"You're even uglier now, maybe not as much inside as out, but getting close."

She paused barely long enough to let her words sink in, vapid and poisonous.

She barely flinched a muscle before hitting me where she knew it would hurt the most.

My heart lay open and unprotected, ready and willing for any attempt to shatter it.

"I've seen you with the hairy bald guy at the mall—you know, the old one," Maria continued, face only inches from mine as she leaned vapidly toward me.

"Now tell me, has little pathetic Emerson finally figured out how to suck it?"

I don't know what happened next exactly. If you asked, I don't even know what I would tell you. Suddenly my hands had grasped her wrists, holding much tighter than I think even I had meant to.

"What the hell is your problem?" I screamed, the words being pounded out furiously between us, her desk teetering beneath the weight of her book bag.

"Do you have any idea how much I hate you? Leave my boyfriend alone, or I swear to God I will make you regret it. Understand?" I shouted.

We were almost on the floor by then. Mr. Williams was frozen against the whiteboard, marker in hand. As if knowing what he had to do next but unsure suddenly as to how to actually do it.

My hands let go ever so slowly. Her pale blue eyes still focused only on mine.

My hands were unsteady as I backed away.

I don't know how I made it out the door without crying, every bone in my body unsure and unsteady.

The hallway was silent and empty.

I couldn't run fast enough, holding my bag tight against my chest. I replayed my words over and over again in my head.

I couldn't even live with myself because of what you did! You tormented me, and for what?

Where did it get you in the end?

The question seeming to linger between us as I stared, the memories of just where it had *started* burning wildly inside my head.

"Hey, turn around for a sec," she had said, her voice like a constant drip now, rather than a snake's terrifying hiss that I had come to know and loathe.

I was fourteen.

I was terrified.

Never knowing just what the years that would follow would bring.

I was completely oblivious to what I had done wrong, if anything.

I waited until the hallways were empty before I started for my locker.

I just wanted to get home, sure that everyone else had left by now, unafraid to make their way toward the busses alongside everyone else.

"*Hey, turn around for a sec,*" *she had asked.*

So I did.

I didn't realize that she wasn't alone until it was far too late. Maria's fifteen-year-old eyes stared ruefully back into mine.

She was all blonde and tall and a perfect size two, everything that every part of me had wanted to be, too—small and beautiful, feminine and fragile.

"God!" she screamed, her high-pitched voice bouncing off the ceiling tiles and recoiling off of a nearby plastic bench.

"She is disgustingly ugly, isn't she?" She laughed again, turning to her friend.

Her friend was an equally pretty girl, a tormentor I did not know.

Maria only glanced back at me for a second, her cruel laughter burning against my ears as she made her way down the hall.

Stopping for a second just in time to look back and see me pull up my pants. It was a pair of my sister's hand-me-downs from Tagman's that didn't quite fit yet.

I never forgot that.

I don't know how long I waited.

I was even unsure of what exactly I was waiting for, the classroom emptying around me with glee.

My eyes focused on every inch of the bathroom stall to which I had been forced to retreat, having made my way down the hall as quickly as I was able. I was sure that at any second Maria was bound to come bursting in with bloodthirsty hands, the ink still fresh on the line on which I had just signed my death sentence.

I jumped a foot out of my skin as my phone buzzed gently against the palm of my hand.

Warren.

It felt like days rather than hours since I had seen him last; he felt impossibly far away.

Why not messaging or nothing? Hate waking up without you now, want you here. Don't wanna go to work

I forced myself to breathe, knowing that I should answer but having no clue as to what to say. The words

Please stay with me

Pathetic, needy, and giving every horrible detail of the last fifteen minutes so easily away, instead choosing to tuck my heart safely and securely away. Instead choosing to hit backspace and delete.

The need for Warren's reassurance suddenly overwhelmed me as I pushed my hair away from my face.

Two pairs of feet scurried past the sinks, laughter shaking me from my reverie.

Their voices were high-pitched and indifferent.

"Hey, Krista, do you think your mom is really going to drop us off at the mall after? I *need* to see Teddy, and Rachel said he usually hangs out there."

"Yeah, but she's going to want me to go home first, though, change and whatnot."

"Change? Why? You look fine," the louder of them demanded, sticking her ass out toward the stall doors as she bent down in front of one of the mirrors, examining every inch of her overly made-up skin.

I pushed my way past them just in time to hear what she had to say next, scornful eyes meeting mine.

"Well, at least we actually *have* dates, unlike some of the pathetic losers they let in this place."

"Hey, writer girl," Krista, the shorter of the two girls, half yelled, daring to turn away from her friend just to make sure that she really had my attention, all half-distracted five furtive seconds of it.

"I like your column," she said and smiled, causing the larger of the two to roll her eyes and groan against the mirror.

It didn't matter though.

"Thanks," I half whispered, starting out of the bathroom and toward my locker, letting my bag slide against my shoulder.

I pulled out my phone despite the fact that there wasn't a single part of me that didn't know better.

I typed furiously against the keyboard, words filling up the little yellow notepad too quickly for the spell-checker to even bother.

They were the thoughts of a girl turned black and white.

Right next to the police blotter were the words *Emmy's Teen Beat*.

Right there so easily, printed more boldly than even I thought necessary.

The girl that had been tormented, tortured, and teased had laid all of her pain out in the open for the entire Riverside world and adjacent to see and to read, daring them just this once, to come on, to come at me.

Chapter 15

"Come on! We'll call it 'Emmy's Teen Beat.' People will love it! Just go with it. Write about whatever makes you mad that day, but keep it professional of course!

"Just make sure that you have it in to me every week by the deadline! Five hundred words every Wednesday by five!"

His words came out in a flurry of overwhelming confusion and pure unsaturated glee.

I had no idea what to say.

"All right, have a good day now. Yup, okay, yeah, good-bye!"

I was out of his office and into the crowded hall before I could even think clearly. The door slammed behind me with impatient fury.

I was fifteen years old and terrified, every naïve bone in my body screaming at me with complete and utter fury.

Writing for yourself is one thing.

Writing for the entire city of Riverside?

That was something else entirely, something that at the time, even I didn't understand, not really.

Every opinion was suddenly open for discussion.

Every thought, feeling, and emotion was now a bullet for those ready and willing to disagree, wielding their rifles fueled by judgments, dead-set ready and aimed.

"'Emmy's Teen Beat' is an embarrassment to our young adults today! Who does this young lady think she is?"

"Someone makes her mad or pokes fun at something she likes, and she thinks she has the right to just pick and choose who she wants to hang out to dry?"

They were right, of course.

I mean, exactly who did I think I was anyway?

I'm sure the idiot who had thrown that stupid grape at me and Kassie sure had a word for me, his debut performance in the weekly newspaper not exactly star-making.

My annoyance exploded into a five-hundred-word column about treating others with respect and doing what your mother told you, including among other things that you should be eating your food instead of playing with it.

All in all and for him at least, it wasn't exactly life-changing, at least not in a good way.

It was almost noon by the time I actually made it to my next class.

Mrs. Everson greeted me ever so kindly as I dared to take my seat, scanning the room for any sort of Maria look-alikes, fully prepared to stop, drop, and roll if necessary.

Mrs. Everson's voice hit me like a cannonball, a dozen small yellow novels atop her dark wooden desk, a computer balanced precariously on the edge.

"The greatest kind of love is tragic."

She was right, of course.

The Romeo and Juliet scenario having been played out in over a dozen movies or more, heartbreak seemed to be one of the things that people most enjoyed seeing.

"We always want what we can't have. Most of the time we don't even know what that is until it's taken away from us."

There was no part of me that wanted to hear this, sure that at any second the ground was going to open from beneath me, sharp teeth scraping against my jeans.

"Didn't they both die in the end anyway?" a voice perked up from a few rows away, squeaky and full of I-just-got-dumped resentment.

"What's the point then? To fall in love and fight the world for it if you just end up alone and dead?"

Even I had to admit that he had a point.

As sad and depressing as it might be, a part of it still rang true.

At least for me.

Oprah's voice filled my head as she coached one young couple versus another on the predicament that desperately trying to earn as much as possible can get you.

Her words echoed against my skull as I glanced at the wallpaper on my phone.

Whether it was love or money, her words still rang true: "You can't take it with you."

The sound of the final bell rang like a beautiful siren in a silent black-and-white world.

I was free.

At least if I wanted to be.

The allure of Tagman's and my dark blue ugly and uncomfortable polyester vest was much easier to resist than one might think. The allure of Warren, however …

His small apartment was a small shelter from the outside world, cozy and warm and safe and comforting.

Every fiber of my body longed for his presence, knowing all the while that I would see him at work regardless.

My feet were heavy against the pavement.

The sky was no longer as clear as it had been the night prior, and fresh snow now dusted the sidewalk.

For once, as I glanced at the large silver bus parked against the sidewalk, walking home seemed like the better option.

It wasn't far from the school to my house, a few blocks if that, but far enough to send shivers up and down my spine the second that I realized I was being followed.

Footsteps fell heavy against the freshly fallen snow, and a body cast a shadow against the snow-filled clouds.

My glance fell on the corner store, an old white building that stood out against the rows and rows of renovated and empty homes, which had windows caked with fingerprints left behind by the lonely and the hopeless. Or both. I couldn't get close enough to find out.

He was on me then, before my body or my mind could comprehend.

Fingernails grasped at the arm of my jacket. A dark face poked out of a dark raincoat tied tight against his jaw.

"Let go of me!" I demanded, pulling against him with all the strength that I could manage.

I only had to pull so far, and then a large set of hands took a sudden hold of him for me.

"Warren!" I breathed, relief flooding through me, the sudden shock of his presence enough to send me flailing backward, fighting to regain my balance.

"Take your hands off of my girlfriend, okay?" he sneered, gripping the would-be bad guy's raincoat tight in the palm of his hand.

"Okay?" he asked again, enunciating the word as if he were speaking to a small child, rather than an apparently deranged individual.

The boy nodded. He swore as he pulled his raincoat from Warren's hands, taking a second to spit on the ground, as if somehow showing his displeasure for not being allowed to do to me whatever it was that he wanted to do.

I felt my body go rigid.

"Fuck you, man!" the kid yelled. He was halfway down the sidewalk already, snow beating against his jacket as he ran.

"I just wanted to talk to her, show her what it's like to fuck a real man, instead of some old worthless bag of shit!"

Warren nearly laughed.

He reached for me as I stumbled and held my arm firmly in his grasp, pulling me along the sidewalk.

"What are you doing out here by yourself exactly? I thought you usually took the bus home."

His questions took on the tone of a federal agent, ready and willing to arrest me for the crime of irritation and attempted self-reliance.

I had to bite my tongue to stop from demanding that he honor my right to have an attorney present at all times.

"I wanted to walk." I shrugged, not an easy feat what with the way he had his arms so close around me, pinning me to his side, allowing no attempt at escape. It was a warm and sexy prison cell.

"What are you doing here anyway?" I stopped suddenly, my voice full of accusations, but lacking the resentment necessary to make them stick the way that they should have.

"It's after three thirty. Shouldn't you be at work? Lifting or moving something? I mean, aren't you going to get in shit for just not showing up for no reason?"

"You never messaged me back."

He said it so casually, as if his explanation should be left at that, no shrugging or sighing or eye rolling, at least not on my part.

I was almost disappointed. I thought he knew me well enough to know that there was no way in hell I was just going to leave it at that.

"You never messaged me back. I got worried, don't want guys like that messing with you when I'm not around."

He shrugged, pulling me closer until my forehead was nearly attached to his shoulder.

"We slept together, Emerson."

He said it so calmly, so matter-of-factly.

My brain was still far too scrambled and unhinged to ever be able to put the words together so easily, to say it, just like that.

"I know," I sighed, allowing my hand to be gripped in his as he pulled me toward an old bus bench, abandoned and covered in cobwebs.

"Well, did you actually think that I could ever actually let anything happen to you after that?"

When I didn't say anything, he kept on, his face now ashen with worry and confusion, dark eyes wide with stress. "Well, I can't, okay? I can't let anything happen to you. I couldn't stand it, not now, not after that."

The bus was a crowded mess by the time we got on it, bodies angled this way and that.

Furtive glances and shifty eyes were dead set on meeting mine as I glanced around for any sign of a face I knew.

All the while, I knew that any hope of spotting a friendly face was in vain; this wasn't my crowd.

The faces that greeted us as Warren pulled me along safely beside him had all aged vigorously.

All I saw were facial piercings and dirt-covered clothes, and worn-out hands that kept accidentally brushing against my skin.

"It's fine," Warren promised, his voice not as reassuring as it should have been, his hands soft against my chin. "Just ignore them."

That was a feat much more than impossible as the bus screeched toward one stop after another, always loading up with more faces unwelcoming and unfamiliar.

One face seemed to catch Warren's attention more than any other—a taller girl, her hair dyed jet-black.

Her lips were redder than rubies as she smiled at him, never even attempting to cover up her partially exposed breasts.

"Hey, Warren!" she exclaimed. "How's it going?"

Her skintight corset was stretched to its limits as she sat down across from us.

Every fiber of my being was suddenly aware of how easily Warren's hand loosened against mine.

"Oh, it's good, I guess." He shrugged, sitting up and pulling away from me ever so slightly. "Just the normal bullshit, you know, working and whatnot. What about you?"

"Meh?" She giggled.

Vomit burned at my throat, desperate to come out, every inch of her exposed skin making me sick to my stomach.

"You should come over sometime. I got a new place I'd really like to show you."

"Yeah, for sure!" Warren smiled, eyes following her as she stood up and hopped off at the nearest stop.

I just wanted to throw up.

"Who was that?" I hardly waited to ask, pulling my arms tight against my chest and scooting against a nearby pole.

"Huh?"

He seemed shell-shocked, as if not truly understanding my question. Who was who? Oh, did you happen to mean that hoochie that I was obviously super into?

Instead of saying any of that, of course, he just shrugged, pulling himself closer against my hip.

I couldn't help but glance out the window to where the slut bag had disappeared to.

Everything about her seemed so opposite of everything that Warren had seemed so desperately to want.

We weren't supposed to fit.

My brain was a scrambled mess as I suddenly started to wonder, glancing at Warren's hands, brushing so gently against mine, white protected by black.

Good and so-called bad.

We weren't supposed to fit.

But we did.

Every fiber of my being wondered suddenly what would happen if in the end, maybe we didn't.

Chapter 16

The house was empty by the time I got home, a note left on the counter informing me that my mother was out grocery shopping and my dad had left for work already.

Angie was the only family member completely MIA. Her whereabouts probably started somewhere around her on-and-off-again boyfriend Luke's bedroom, and ended with the classiest of tissues in his bathroom.

Warren was quieter than usual as he followed me around the house.

He waited in the hall outside my bedroom as I changed and sat silently across from me at the kitchen table, eyeing me suspiciously.

He seemed to know the questions that burned furiously in the back of my mind.

I had to keep eating to resist the urge to scratch out his kind, deep brown eyes.

"She's just a friend, Emerson," he sighed, seemingly tired of this game before we had even started playing.

"A friend who forgot to put on a shirt this morning?" I asked, my voice coming out meaner than I had intended. The feeling of his fingers loosening against mine was still fresh as fire in the back of my mind.

"A friend who then had no problem shoving her boobs in my boyfriend's face?"

Warren simply stared, as silent as ever.

"Nicki," he said suddenly, standing up from the table and following my trail of cereal all the way to the sink.

"Some chick I met online a few years ago."

It was impossible as he talked not to notice the strange nervous edge to his voice. It seemed to bounce off every inch of the countertop and violently back at me, smacking me in the face as if demanding that I wake up already.

"Can we go now? I'm in enough trouble as it is for not showing up and not calling and shit. Rather get to work before eleven o'clock."

He was so sarcastic I decided not to fight him on it, pressing my lips as I pushed my bowl toward the center of the already cluttered table and stood up.

It was almost five thirty by the time the next bus rolled around.

My shift didn't start for at least another hour or so.

I kept waiting for Warren to say something, for him to smile and take my hand like normal.

I kept waiting.

The entire twenty-minute bus ride was spent in awkward silence.

His eyes focused everywhere and anywhere, it seemed, as long as he wasn't looking at me.

I kept waiting.

The bus lurched to a stop with all the suave maneuvering of a minivan, the driver and seats loaded up with coke.

My heart fluttered as I felt Warren's arm brush against mine, his fingers tight against my sleeve as we crossed the busy street.

I kept waiting.

I was waiting for him to turn and kiss me on the cheek, my jaw, or my eyes, any part of me that he could reach.

I kept waiting.

My lungs drained as I watched him walk swiftly through the front doors that led to Tagman's hell on earth. Without so much as a glance behind him as he walked swiftly and smoothly away from me, without so much as a glance or a good-bye kiss.

My eyes burned with worry, and I kept waiting.

Every fiber of my being screamed with panic as I choked back the hysteria that threatened to overwhelm me completely, clawing at my bones and leaving my skin singed and burning. All I could do was hope as I made my way toward the back, purse held tight against my chest, that whatever had just happened could easily be taken back, that there was no part of him so willing to simply leave me, to leave us, at that.

It was a nuthouse by the time I finally made it up front, of course, Tommy hollering about things this way and that.

His blond hair seemed permanently messed up. His skinny jeans now dropped far below an even blonder butt crack.

I kept waiting as I pushed my way through a mosh pit toward my till, glancing at my phone, hoping that Warren was going to come around, that he had to.

My worry slowly gave way to rage as night turned from day, the mosh pit refusing to thin out, even just a little.

My phone was unmoving and silent in my pocket.

I was unable to stop my heart from fluttering in my chest as I felt a pair of hands brush against my back.

It was only Tommy, of course, signaling a seemingly super-secret money drop-off of loonies and fives.

We really needed lives.

The world slowed to a stop as my lunchtime finally rolled around. My guts twisted inside themselves as I made my way through the staff-only doors and toward my locker.

I knew I had to do something.

My feet were heavy against the pale-painted concrete as I pushed my way past boxes and skids. Receiving seemed miles away.

He was there, of course, all muscles, black T-shirt, and faded black jeans, his sweat-covered tattoos glistening in the fluorescent lighting.

My glance fell on Joel's disapproving gaze as I stepped my way through a mess of boxes and milk crates.

"You're going to get yourself killed, you know?" Warren sighed, reaching for me, hands grazing my fingertips as I felt the wood give way from beneath me.

The cold concrete floor was suddenly a lot less inviting as I felt myself plummet toward it.

"Jesus!" Warren screamed, falling over himself as his hands found my waist, my arms now scraped and bloody.

"I'm sorry," I said, the stinging sensation burning tears against my eyelids as I fought to control them.

Warren's hands were strong and warm as he fought to hold and steady me, lifting me against his chest.

"Dude, come on, get the bitch out of here, okay?" one of the newer guys yelled.

His impatience seemed to be shared by the rest of the group.

"Yeah, man, we got stuff to do," Joel said. He just had to chime in, his voice tinged with the slightest bit of worry as he saw my bloody arm, blood that had smeared against Warren's face and neck.

"She's my girlfriend, you asshole," Warren screamed back. "She got hurt 'cause you morons have to leave shit everywhere, and if I ever hear you call her a bitch again, *ever*, you'll fucking regret it, understand?"

We were gone before the redheaded kid could dare to say something back.

Warren's shy demeanor seemed to disappear completely the second I was in jeopardy, even if jeopardy just meant a few stitches and a bruise.

The first-aid room door swung open violently with our presence. My eyes focused on one thing and one thing only: the plastic-covered bedspread.

Warren was seemingly oblivious to my ideas as he set me down against the plastic-covered pillow.

He closed the door gently with his foot as he dug around for Band-Aids and anti-infectant.

My mouth ran dry as I tried desperately for something to say, glancing down at my bloodied uniform. The word *sexy* never seemed further away.

I watched in awkward, awed silence as he dug around, moving from one cupboard to the other.

"Warren?" I whispered, daring to grasp his attention but at a loss to know how to keep it.

Seducing men had never been one of my strong suits, despite the fact that the only man who had ever seen me naked was standing less than a foot away, right within arm's reach.

He merely grunted before pulling out a large white tin labeled "FIRST AID," dropping it onto the plastic-covered mattress in front of me with ease.

"Here, hold this," he ordered.

Avoiding eye contact, I did as I was told.

He took the small bundle of tape, scissors, and gauze, sighing as he reached back into the tin for my Band-Aids.

"I'm fine, you know." I lied, pulling myself upright so that we were now face-to-face, knee-to-knee, his lips mere inches from mine.

"I told you not to come back there, you know?" he mumbled, completely ignoring me.

"Not when those idiots leave crap everywhere. Not with how klutzy you are.

"I mean, how many times do I have to tell you I love you? Tell you that I don't want anything happening to you?

"And by anything, I really do mean anything, even this. Goddamn it, Emerson, you're going to be the death of me."

"Kiss me," I whispered, dropping the gauze and scissors onto the floor, not caring how loud they clattered against the concrete when they got there, not caring who heard.

"Emerson," he sighed, eyes finally meeting mine after what felt like days.

His coldness during the last twenty-four hours was not forgotten. It lingered in the back of my mind like poison, a rattrap, wide open and tempting.

"Kiss me?" I asked again, pulling myself closer toward him, chest against his, my lips against his neck.

"Kiss me," I said.

So he did.

The small bed seemed to cower beneath us as my back hit the plastic, legs wrapped in and around his.

His hands were against my back, my hips, any part of me that he could get at.

I love him was the only thing that I could think, even if I didn't truly know what that meant yet.

I think that he did.

Chapter 17

It was almost ten thirty by the time I got home, digging through my purse as I attempted to comb out what was left of my ponytail.

I took my sweet time as I searched for my keys. The last thing I needed my parents to see was a hickey.

Angie was still awake, of course. Her entire corner of our basement was lit up by whatever mind-boggling gossip she had decided to obsess about this week.

"Can you turn the TV down at least?" I asked as I stripped down to my underwear before quickly changing into my pajamas.

I was unable to stop myself from glancing over my shoulder as some blue-eyed, blonde-haired reporter planted herself right in the middle of Hollywood Boulevard, a makeshift memorial to some heartthrob celebrity just barely visible over her left shoulder.

"It's just so sad!" Angie squealed, smacking herself in the face with a handful of tissues, trying to dry her tear-dampened cheeks.

"Were you guys close?" I couldn't stop myself from asking, the acid dripping out of my throat like a tap someone had left on.

"Goddamn it, Emerson! He was only our favorite actor growing up, don't you remember?"

I didn't actually.

I didn't say that, though, instead choosing to pretend the way she said *"ours"* was way too distracting.

Not hers, or mine, or probably yours, but ours.

The thought of *anything* that Angie and I had ever shared was nearly mind-bending. The queen bee and the disinterested, maybe even more unmixable than Kassie and me.

I made sure to grab my phone before I dared to join her, scared that at the last second, the drawbridge would start to close, with me inside of it, no less.

Her pink castle was nearly impenetrable, seemingly surrounded by a moat and an electric fence. There was no way to get inside without being let in.

"So, how'd it happen?" I dared to ask, reaching for the pinkest of all blankets to cover up my feet, providing an obligatory glance toward the TV.

"Drugs, of course." She sniffled, as if I were a complete idiot for asking such a thing, which when I thought about it, wasn't so far off base.

The whole idiot thing, I mean, 'cause really, how *else* do famous people die nowadays?

"They found him alone in his hotel room." Angie shrugged, recapping what I'm sure the news reporter had said only minutes prior.

Only this time with more dramatics. "What a waste, you know?" She cried, reaching for another box of tissues. "He was only like thirty something, I think."

Okay, that was it; I'd had enough.

I was unable to cry over someone that I never had truly known, when I had lost someone so close not too long ago.

I barely made it a foot before her words stopped me dead in my tracks, the name *Warren* floating so easily off her overglossed, stuck-out lips.

"You slept with him, didn't you?" she asked, no longer in need of hot tea or a warm blanket, staring at me with tearless eyes as her voice stayed flat, matter-of-fact, as if she already knew the answer to a question that she had absolutely no right to ask.

"Emerson?" she whispered.

My eyes now closed against the flashing TV screen, my hands reaching out for the door handle—something, anything to hold onto.

"It's okay! I won't tell anyone," she promised, her voice dropping as she shrugged, her eyes falling to the floor, as the truth seemed to flow effortlessly out of her.

"After all, you're almost eighteen, right? Technically you can do whatever you want."

She was right, of course, if by *almost* she meant *almost* in two and a half months from now.

"Just be careful, okay?" she said, her voice taking on a tone of seriousness that I was so far from used to, it actually freaked me out a little.

"Careful of what exactly?" I asked, knowing what she was getting at but unwilling to go there alone.

"Just be careful."

It was impossible not to notice the way her voice picked up at the end, her long brown hair swinging back effortlessly into a ponytail, pale eyes turned toward the TV.

As if she felt bad for me. Too bad to say what really needed to be said, words that hung so desperately in the frosty air that lingered between us.

My thoughts were tangled and incoherent as I tucked myself into bed, leaving my phone silent and half dead on the bedside table. I was unwilling to plug it in and willing it to die completely.

I needed silence.

I needed to get away.

Just this once.

Please?

The darkness overwhelmed me with ease, silent and unrelenting.

A boy's face flashed violently in the back of my mind, kind eyes meeting mine. His smile turned cold easily with the words of a girl, a girl I didn't even know.

Her laughter burned against me as I tried desperately to open my eyes, the kind-eyed boy holding me down, pinning me to the ground.

Sunrise flooded my room, illuminating the backs of my eyelids in a strange auburn glow.

I so didn't want to get up now.

The promise of another day at Riverside wasn't exactly overwhelming, at least not in a good way.

My nightmare clung to me like a giant spiderweb full of giant flesh-eating tarantulas, clinging at me, worrying at my body, biting at my skin.

The boy's kind eyes were now swollen and red, his smile turned sinister, twisted with the words of a girl.

Angie was gone by the time I got dressed, of course, her room a perfect disaster of bright pinks and burning reds, as if good old St. Valentine had literally gotten sick on her bedspread, vomiting up hearts and roses.

My mom's voice welcomed me from the top of the stairs, the smell of waffles and peanut butter very nearly making my mouth water.

My mind was suddenly unable to recall the last thing I had eaten that wasn't coated in sugar or some morphed candy gummy bear.

My feet were heavy against the hardwood as I made my way up the stairs, dropping my phone and purse against the linoleum without a second thought.

It was impossible while being so close to Mom to not tell her every tantalizing detail of the last forty-eight hours.

Her warm brown eyes met mine over a large cup of fresh coffee; her smile was unbiased and kind.

The words slipped out faster than I could say them, my mind retracing every step in an attempt to unsay what I was about to say next: "I slept with him."

She started, blinking back at me for a few seconds, seemingly at a loss for words, then quietly asked, "Warren?"

I shrugged, as if there were anyone else that I could be talking about, a thug or a gangster perhaps. Maybe both, at the same time. I almost laughed. I had to bite my lip to stop myself, nerves threatening to overtake me completely.

I was a complete mess. My eyes welled up as she stared, tears threatening to boil over.

Her expression of laughter sent shock waves of panic up and down my spine.

"Why are you crying?" She laughed. "It's okay!"

It was?

How in the hell was this okay?

Her teenage daughter admitting to showing much more than her hoo-ha to a much older man?

Bra and all, coming off, just like that?

I kept bracing for a rage that I feared would never come, her face reddened from tears derived from laughter instead of sadness or fear.

"You're happy, right?" she asked, seeming to find a second long enough to breathe. "You're happy, and he loves you. You were safe, right? And he was good about everything?"

I nodded, taking the time to think it over carefully, running the last few days over in my mind.

His hands warm against mine, arms wrapped around my waist, lips at my neck, my jaw, any part of me that he could get at.

"That's all that matters to me." She shrugged, dropping a plate of warm waffles and a glass of perfectly cold milk right within arm's reach.

"As long as he loves you and you love him and you're not doing it for any other reason than that, as long as you're ready and he would never force you either way, that's all that matters to me, really, as long as you're safe."

I was in shock, seriously.

Tears of joy and confusion threatened to overwhelm me completely. I had to force myself to breathe.

It's okay!

I couldn't control myself any longer.

Nearly taking the waffles and milk jug with me, I leaped across the counter, hugging her to me with all the force that we could handle. The tears I had been fighting now flowed freely down my cheeks.

Never had I been happier that Angie wasn't around to judge or harass me.

I was sure that my bawling put her previous night's cry fest to shame quite easily.

My mom seemed just as embarrassed as I was as she pried herself from my dampened grasp.

The toaster was screeching painfully, the smoke alarm chiming in with backup vocals.

I don't know how long we had stayed like that—probably long enough to make me late for school.

Not that it mattered.

At least it wouldn't for a while.

Our laughter was enough to send Ruffles and Cinnamon running for cover, bouncing off the yellow-painted walls and vibrating against the table.

I could only hope, as the morning sunshine shone easily through the open windows, that the pain of laughter vibrating against my skull, radiating in my bones, would be greater than the pain of needing someone much more desperately than I had ever given myself permission to.

The pain of love, the pain of loss, aching simultaneously. Like a bullet that goes straight through the heart.

I was doomed the day that I met him, whether I ever realized it or not, for better or worse, through sickness and in health, through good times and in bad, even if I didn't truly know what that meant yet.

Chapter 18

My mom blasted the radio all the way to school, the Heartbreakers screaming out one of their more popular melodies about love and tragedy.

I hadn't been this comfortable with her in weeks.

I loved it.

I barely noticed the sound of cruel laughter as she pulled against the curb, all of the windows rolled down, allowing what remained of the sunshine to swallow us whole.

"Why if it isn't Emerson!" the cruel voice reveled, high-pitched and more annoying than ever. "The biggest slut in town."

It was Rebecca, of course, her tone making me wonder just how long it had taken this particular case of sour grapes to settle over.

"Oh, man," I sighed, feigning shock and disappointment, turning so that we were face-to-face, eye-to-eye, and ear-to-ear.

"I don't know why you didn't run this year, Becks. I mean you wish every year, don't you?" I shrugged, shaking my head. "The boys of Riverside are going to be disappointed, you know?"

I almost laughed, watching as her face reddened and her posse smiled, petite shoulders lifting with fury.

"*You little bitch!*" Rebecca screeched, right up in my face.

"I know you know that Warren wants me, not you," she started, seemingly on a roll. Like a steam roller trying to outrun its power cord.

"Not that skanky little bitch I saw you both talking to yesterday, but *me*! He only slept with you to make *me* jealous! Yeah, that's right; I know you guys did it!"

I could only stare in horrified amusement, aware of the overjoyed crowd that had started to gather around us, thrilled with the fact that they might actually get to see some serious girl-on-girl action.

If by girl-on-girl they meant hairpulling and serious R-rated swearing, that is.

"God, do you even hear yourself?" I demanded, sure that at any second, a full-on fight was about to break out, anger boiling dangerously in my veins.

"Warren doesn't want you, okay? He just doesn't! If he did, he would be with you! I mean, what guy is going to use *me*, the plus-sized blonde girl, to make *you*, the small petite annoying little brunette, jealous? Like, seriously? Who does that?"

She just stared, seemingly at a complete loss for words.

My heart pounded furiously as I fought to catch my breath, glancing around for any means of escape.

"He loves me, okay?"

It was the first time I had ever said the words out loud, and they felt foreign against my tongue.

"He loves me."

I had to say it again, just for good measure, just to hear the words that had tormented me so easily.

Does he?

Doesn't he?

If he does, does he really?

"Fine," she sneered, fury-filled shoulders loosening up just a bit, skin now almost more tan than red. "Fine. You want to believe that, Emerson, go ahead." She shrugged, stuffing her perfectly manicured nails inside designer pockets.

"Just don't come crying to me when you finally open your eyes to the fact that this entire time, the world has been trying to tell you otherwise."

She was gone then, a fading shadow against the fading snow, the ground dry for the first time in what felt like decades, her words echoing in the distance that lingered between us.

I made my way to my locker in a haze, swallowing the aftertaste of her words like battery acid, scorching my throat on the way down, my feet seeming to move in slow motion.

Her eyes burned fiercely in the back of my mind, a rage far too strong to ever be consumed.

Her words burned at my insides, leaving my gut a twisted and rotted mess.

My own words scorched us both.

Good versus bad.

My knight in shining armor, passed out and oblivious of the danger his damsel had just inflicted on the Wicked Witch of the West.

My phone was like lava in the palm of my hand.

Dude!

I typed furiously, angling myself against a wall in the restroom, out of mind and out of sight.

I know you're asleep and I really hope that this doesn't wake you up and I'm sorry if it does but I just totally YELLED AT REBECCA in front of like everyone!

She was flipping out saying how you wanted to be with her and not me and that you're only using me to make her jealous and she kept screaming about how she knows it!

I totally told her off!

I hit send with all the subtlety of a puma lion, paws and claws unable to contain my excitement, waiting impatiently for his reply.

I hammered my fists against one of the vacant stall doors, silently screeching, *I did it!*

The feeling of my phone buzzing against my hand was enough to send me nearly falling over backward.

His reply left a lot to be desired.

Good I guess.

I swear he shrugged. The feeling of his eyes seeming to stare right past me was almost more than I could take.

His message continued.

Trying to sleep though,

Got to work in a few hours you know.

Fine! I internally screamed, smashing the words against the keyboard before backpedaling toward erase.

Subconsciously I bashed my idiocy.

Of course, he didn't care.

Why would he?

It's not like she hadn't spent *months* torturing us, a girl so close to evil her own parents should have felt compelled to warn the public.

She twisted Warren's words inside and out with every chance she could get and attempted at any and all times possible to completely sabotage the both of us.

It's not like that had meant anything to me, right?

It's not like I had spent countless sleepless nights wide-awake and terrified, tears welling up against my eyelashes and threatening to overwhelm me completely, right?

It's not like just this once I had needed him to be there with me, more than anything else, right?

Needed him to acknowledge that what I had said and done was warranted, after everything she had said and done to the both of us in comparison.

It's not like that should have meant something to him, right?

My own fury burned wildly in my veins.

Yup, I thought so too.

Chapter 19

I had completely lost track of time by the time that my first class rolled around.

Charts and beakers were not exactly doing it for me today, so I decided instead to take advantage of our school's trust thy student system, meaning that I could pretty much wander around the halls as much as I wanted and no one would say anything.

My mind led me to the cafeteria, quiet and almost completely abandoned.

The allure of French fries at eight thirty in the morning was far too much for my haggard self to resist.

I needed comfort food, maybe right now more than ever.

I forced myself to sit down as I stuffed the delicious grease-soaked golden arches in my mouth, to actually sort out everything that had happened in the last few months or so.

Losing my virginity—in more ways than one.

My brain not fully able to function at the idea of being so close to a naked man—and a hairy one at that!

His warm hands were like fire against my pale, nervous, terrified skin, steadying me when I was unable to steady myself—warm, safe, and comforting.

My own thoughts were a tangled and incoherent mess, his voice like a fire alarm in the silence.

"I love you, Emerson."

Eyes kind and patient.

"Be mine?"

His voice was like hot lava against my skin, melting any and all of my inhibitions. Which was much easier than it should have been.

I couldn't think when I was around him, not even a little bit, not at all, not even for a second.

My memories shook like a gavel slamming down onto a judge's desk, vibrating against my skin.

Suddenly pale eyes met mine with the first kindness I felt like I had seen in days—Kassie.

It felt like decades instead of just a few days since I had seen her last, her hair now a blonde bob of swirling colors aimed this way and that.

Her heart-shaped face was full of flurry and excitement as she plopped herself down across from me.

She slammed her purse the size of a small suitcase against the table with all the force of a bowling ball.

"Thank God you're actually here today!" she squealed. "I have the greatest idea ever that I've been trying to tell you for days, which I would have told you already, you know, if you weren't *too busy* for me!"

She laughed as she said it, but still, it wasn't hard to see the dabs of hurt that lined her eyes.

"Still!" she exclaimed, cutting me off before I could even start to apologize, sure that I wouldn't be finished for at least a few hours, if not days.

"Since you both seem to have forgotten, you and that Warren guy who likes to steal you from me, it is almost, my dear, your one-year anniversary!

"That's right. You guys have officially been making googly eyes at each other and making out for well over eleven months now."

We had?

Really?

That didn't make sense.

My brain racked itself for a time line—our first kiss, the first time we talked, the day that *I* asked him *out*.

There was no way that that had all happened almost a year ago. Had it?

Like really?

It seemed like only yesterday that we were coached for spending too much time together at work.

His attention was more than overly focused on me as I made my way past receiving, making sure to look at the ground as I walked, aware with every sense of my soul that someone was watching me, someone whom I occasionally liked to watch back.

How had we gone from that, to this?

My temper threatened to overwhelm me as I glanced at my phone for what felt like the one hundred thousandth time since the first bell had rung.

His words had burned a hole through my insides, leaving my heart a totaled mess.

I didn't say any of this, of course, to Kassie at least.

I just smiled and nodded.

I was sure that I was overreacting, at least a little bit. Every couple fights, right?

I know I wouldn't be all that charming if someone had decided to wake me up when I had only managed to get a few hours of sleep to begin with.

Still.

Kassie's voice dragged me from my reverie as she squealed, excitement threatening to boil over and soak us both completely.

"What?" I asked, flabbergasted.

"I have like the best idea ever!" she screamed. "Let's surprise him!

"Well, not us exactly, since I don't think he's into me like that, but I'll help you cook, and we'll surprise him with this awesome home-cooked meal for when he gets home later and you can be there all sexy and whatever!"

I nodded and smiled, still the slightest bit skeptical, unsure how after our last text messages, a surprise "here I am" homecoming meal would actually go over.

I only wish that I had known, as she dragged me away from my comfort food and down the hall, how the *greatest surprise ever* (her words) would end up being the end of everything that I had come to hold near and dear.

Chapter 20

We drove to Warren's house with the windows rolled down, the air perfectly warm for the first time in what felt like weeks. What was left of the snow and the ice had seemingly disappeared, fading and melting away.

We made sure to stop at the local grocery store just long enough to grab a large box of Kraft dinner and a few boxes of Hamburger Helper. Gourmet chefs we had never claimed to be.

We timed it perfectly enough that we missed Warren's bus by mere seconds.

Kassie was unable to control herself as she leaned out the window, waving erratically.

Screaming at the top of her lungs, she parked against the curb, blonde hair glowing and haphazard.

"Good-bye, Warren!" she squealed, laughter filling her throat as she spoke, ignoring any and all attempts to pull her back into the still-running vehicle.

She finally gave in only as the bus vanished around the corner, every fiber of my being praying that Warren's headphones had been in already.

Kind eyes turned away as my best friend did what best friends do better than anyone else: act like complete and total loony tunes.

Balancing milk on my knee, I bent toward the small welcome mat constantly lingering just steps outside of Warren's apartment. Every cliché was laid open and oblivious in front of me as I reached for his key.

His place was pitch-black of course, the only light creeping in around the corners of his partially closed drapes.

The counters were partially covered with half-empty energy drinks, just like always.

Aside from my own bedroom, there was no place in the world where I felt so safe.

Safe yet terrified. I'd never been in Warren's place without him, without his constant guidance and protection as I reached for this and that.

Kassie was more than ready to start exploring the place.

Eyes intent on his bedroom door, she made her way down the hall and past the living room.

I had no idea how to stop her.

"Oh, what's this?" she asked, her voice rising just a tad at the word *this*.

As I attempted to turn on the stove, sure that I was about to get burned one way or another, I dared to ask, "What's what?" sure that I was about to regret it.

I felt my face turn red as she smiled, holding a small package of condoms on the very tip of her finger, as if prepared to throw them in the air.

"What's this?"

I laughed, fighting my embarrassment.

"You missed that day in health class?" she almost spit, choosing instead to toss the dramatic evidence of an apparent conquest at my chest.

It only took a few trips to get everything inside. We dipped into the bags that now littered the kitchen counter, grabbing the milk and tossing the butter.

We hit play on her iPod as we cooked, the sound of Pink filling the kitchen, the anger-fueled voice bouncing against the kitchen tiles and vibrating off the pots and pans.

My glance fell on my phone as it sat silent, unmoving and unused for what felt like days but was probably (as Kassie kept reminding me) only a few minutes.

I was worried that Warren's reaction to this break-and-enter fest wouldn't be exactly what either Kassie or I expected.

The time ticked painfully by.

The smell of overcooked cheese burned at me, milk gone stagnant an arm's length away.

Kassie's voice shook at me, her screeching laughter overwhelming as she juggled a pot of boiling water, noodles threatening to boil over.

My own heart pounded violently against my chest as I tried desperately to avoid scalding all ten of my fingers.

I heard it then, the smallest of sounds, a beep, like a forgotten alarm or a pocket watch. Just a beep, not enough to send my heart falling to my knees.

My breath was slow and rapid as the pain of months on end burned at me, scalding my veins and leaving my skin torched and bleeding.

It was just a beep.

"Hey, hold on," I called, laughing as I made my way toward Warren's computer, all black and shiny, as high-tech and as complicated as it could get.

My hand touched the mouse just enough to send the screen flashing violently back at me, colors twisted beautifully.

A series of missed messages and tweets, forgotten e-mails and IMs, were all right there.

Words like *Hey baby* all bright pink and lying right out in the open, begging for me to see and read.

Right out in the open,

God I miss you, he typed, the letters furious and flashy.

Her name is Emerson.

We work together kind of likes me I guess but we haven't fucked or anything yet

His explanation hit me like a rock, the words rolling over me like a stream roller, burning my skin and singeing at my tears.

She's okay kind of nagging and stuff, also kind of young for me I mean she's like sixteen or something I think

I'll take whatever I can get at this point?

Know what I mean?

I snapped back, Kassie's voice claiming my attention, laced with panic and concern.

Emerson?

I think she called.

I couldn't quite hear her.

Emerson look at me!

What's going on?

Emerson?!

I wanted to answer.

I even tried.

My hands found the cold floor so suddenly that it hurt, my knees buckling from beneath me.

I wanted to answer her; I even tried to find the words, my lungs seeming to fill with water, as wetness boiled against my eyelashes.

Tears staining my skin, burning at my lips.

I wanted to answer, but I couldn't find the words, sure that I would have to figure out how to breathe first.